Clayton

Clayton

BOURBON & BLOOD
Book Two

CHASITY BOWLIN

Clayton
Paperback Edition
Copyright © 2025 by Chasity Bowlin

Love N. Books Press
An Imprint of Wolfpack Publishing
1707 E. Diana Street
Tampa, FL 33610

www.lovenbookspress.com

Cover design by Jennilynn Wyer Designs
Edited by My Brother's Editor

Clayton was originally self-published in 2024 by Chasity Bowlin.

Paperback ISBN 979-8-89567-118-4
Ebook ISBN 979-8-89567-117-7
LCCN 2025937443

Clayton

Prologue

I know something is wrong. The house is dark. The cartoons or music that Emma Grace loves aren't blaring from her bedroom. It's just after eight in the evening. At the very least, I should hear Annalee arguing with her that it's bedtime. But there's nothing. The house is so quiet that it feels unnatural.

I bypass the den and head straight to the kitchen where I can see light. Annalee stands at the counter, her back to the door. Her hair is pulled back in a simple pony-tail, but it bares the curve of her neck. God, I want to taste that. I want to bury my face against her neck and inhale the scent of her. But I haven't laid hands on her in so long, I'm not sure I'd even be permitted. *My choice,* I remind myself. I know I've made it for the right reasons, and a part of me still believes, deep down, that what I'm doing is for the best. Another part of me wants to tell her every-thing and wash my hands of it all.

By virtue of being a Darcy, I'm a good liar. We've made our fortunes on that for generations, but I can't lie to her, and I know it. That would make me no better than him. So for months, I've just avoided her. Coming home late. Leaving early. Locking myself in my office when I am at home. I've put so much distance between us that I don't know if it can ever be bridged.

"Where's Emma Grace?" I ask. Our daughter is a safe topic at least.

Annalee turns back to look at me. She's been crying, though she's applied makeup and tried to camouflage it. *I did that.* Every tear she sheds right now is my fault. But I can't change course. It's too late for that now. I have to stop Samuel no matter what it costs. Too many people are counting on me, including Annalee, even though she doesn't know it yet.

"She's at a sleepover. I thought that was for the best..." She pauses, takes a deep breath, and then traps me with a cold, steady gaze. "We need to talk, Clayton."

The most dreaded words in the English language. Fuck. "Do we have to do this tonight? It's been a hell of a day, Ann," I hedge.

"Yes," she replies, arms crossed over her chest and her chin up like she's daring me to take a swing at her. I never have. I never would. But I know with the way she grew up, part of her still expects it to happen.

I put my briefcase on the counter and grab a beer from the fridge. I'm being a dick and I know it. If I could have just a little more time, I could get it all back to normal. I could take her away somewhere for the weekend and make up for the last six months of isolation. "You wanted to talk," I say to her, my tone sharp. "So talk."

"Tell me what you're hiding," she says.

I can't do that. I could, but I need for her to be able to deny having any knowledge of what I'm up to if shit goes south. It's the only way to keep her and Emma Grace safe. "I'm not hiding anything. I'm just busy with work. The

2

distillery is in the fucking toilet thanks to my asshole of a father...it's not going to do a one-eighty and turn a profit by itself, Annalee."

Her glare tells me she's not buying it. Not that I expected her to. She's nobody's fool.

"Tell me the truth, Clayton, or you're moving out."

I set the beer down on the counter. "You're not kicking me out of my own house."

She's pacing the kitchen, her hands clenched at her sides. "You're never here anyway," she shoots back. "You're gone when I get up in the morning and you don't even come into our bedroom until you know I'm asleep. You haven't touched me in months, Clayton...not since you went to Japan."

How can I tell her that I can't face her? That lying to her and hiding things from her is eating me up inside. So much that I can't even stand for her to look at me? "Annalee, you're overreacting. In a few months, things will go back to normal. The distillery will be on firmer footing and—"

"Don't," she interrupts. "You and I both know this isn't just about you being busy at Fire Creek. You're hiding something, Clayton. You're lying to me...and you either tell me what it is, or you get out."

"Then I guess I should pack," I reply, hoping she's bluffing.

She makes a sound that cuts me to the quick. I'm reminded of a line from a Jason Isbell song, about the sound a woman makes as her heart begins to break. I always wondered what that sounded like. Now I know.

I can see the hurt in her eyes, in the slight tremble of her lip and the firming of her jaw. Never one for theatrics or wasted emotion, the mask falls into place again immediately. "Do you even care?" she asks. "Or is this what you

3

wanted? Did you just grow progressively colder and more distant in the hopes that I'd give you the out you wanted without you having to be the bad guy?"

I can't answer that. I can't answer anything. Telling her the truth is out of the question and adding to the bitter tasting lies I've already told, even if they were by omission, isn't a line I'm willing to cross. "I'll go. We don't have to fight about it."

She screams like a wounded animal. I duck as a glass comes flying at my head. Other various pieces of cutlery and a few dishes follow. Crossing the room, I grab her arms, holding them down to her sides. I lock my arms around her and I know, in that second, that this might be the last time I ever hold her.

"Annalee, stop! Just stop!" I whisper against her ear. My voice sounds unfamiliar inside my own head. That broken and desperate plea sounds like it belongs to someone else.

"Don't tell me what to do, you son of a bitch!" The words come out of her like the sounds of a hissing cat—low, angry, with a growl to them that conveys just how dangerous she is in the moment.

I've never seen her like this. Not once in the twelve years since I've known her has she lost it like this. Another cross to bear, another crime to lay at my door. We've fought in the past, but it was always stupid, and more often than not just an excuse to get to the makeup sex. This is the first time we've ever really laid into one another this way. All I want is to tell her the truth, to make the hurt go away, but I can't. Not yet. Not until it's all done.

I've broken more laws on a daily basis, every day for the last six months, than I had previously in all my life. I've lied. I've stolen. I've broken into my father's apartment more than once. I've extorted information from his

4

mistresses, every one of them. I've threatened, coerced, bribed judges and cops. I've tapped his phone and bugged his house. And if those things don't get me what I need, I've accepted that I might even have to kill the bastard. I'm not as conflicted about any of that as I am about this, about letting her go to keep her safe from the consequences of my actions.

"I'm going to a lawyer," she says on a broken sob. "I want a divorce."

"I'll give it to you," I tell her. It feels like something was just cut out of me, without anesthesia, like I ought to be bleeding from the wound.

"Is it another woman?" she asks, her voice so low, so broken, that it's hard to hear.

I shake my head. I won't tell that lie. There's never been another woman, not since the moment I laid eyes on her. I won't sully what we've had by saying otherwise. "No, Ann. It's not like that...we're just not the same people we used to be." It's the closest thing to the truth I can tell her. I'm not the man she married. I'm not the do-gooder, upright, cross every T and dot every I, man who would do whatever it took not to be like his father. Instead, I'm becoming just like him. It's the only way to bring him down.

"Get out. Just get out." She sounds defeated, but not broken. Annalee will never be broken, not by me or anyone else. It's probably why I fell in love with her.

I let go of her. "I'll come get my things tomorrow while you're out."

"They'll be on the lawn. Leave your key," she says coolly.

I don't answer. I just turn and walk out while I have the strength to. I'm going to burn for what I have to do to Samuel Darcy, one way or another. Whether I ruin him financially or socially, whether I have to cross that line and end him like the diseased animal he is, there will be a reckoning for it...a price to pay. If I'm out of her life, she'll be safe from it and she'll be there to keep our daughter safe. It's cold comfort, but it's all I've got.

One

CLAYTON

(SIX MONTHS LATER)

I t's not a good morning. After spending half the night pouring over my asshat father's bank records and reviewing the files from the attorney that were not actually supposed to be given to me, I'm under the gun. If I don't get Samuel to give up guardianship of my mother before the next portion of her trust matures, it's over.

He's blown through millions already, spending her money on disposable women and keeping up his image as southern aristocracy. None of it has been used to provide for her care. That's been Mia, Quentin and myself working our asses off to pay for her caregivers. But we're drowning. We can't keep it up. And if he gets his hands on this, the only option left will be to put her in a nursing home. That is *not* going to fucking happen.

With my tie hanging loose and my jacket draped over my arm, I grab my briefcase and open the front door. Immediately, I stop. My morning went from being bad to being blown straight to hell. My soon-to-be ex-wife is standing on my doorstep, her hand raised as she was about to knock.

"I'm sorry I didn't call," she says, like we're polite strangers. "I was hoping to catch you before you left for work."

Clearly she did. The fact that I'm standing there is all the confirmation she needs. I'm usually pretty good at keeping the anger at a simmer. There's nothing happening between the two of us that isn't a direct result of all that I've done. I know that, but when you're hurting, those kinds of rational thoughts just aren't as satisfying as being a total dick.

"Why?" That's as close to civil as I can get.

She blinks at me. "I need you to pick Emma Grace up after school. I have to go to Louisville this afternoon."

"You could have texted that."

Her lips firm and a little line appears between her brows. I used to piss her off on purpose, pick a fight just to get the amazing make-up sex. There's no percentage in it now, but old habits die hard.

She steps inside the door and shuts it softly behind her. "Clayton, I know this isn't easy, but do we really have to snap at each other like this?"

So on top of being stressed, angry, hurt, now I get to feel guilty, too. Fan-fucking-tastic. "You're right. I'm sorry. I'm just in a shit mood. Yes, I will pick up Emma Grace after school."

"Thank you," she replies. "I won't be home until around nine or so. If you want, she can just stay the night here."

"That's fine. I'll drop her off at school in the morning." Look at us. Being all reasonable and adult-like. Son of a bitch.

I realize that something isn't quite right with Annalee. She looks nervous. And she hates driving in Louisville. She wouldn't go there without a damned good reason.

"Is everything okay? You only ever go to Louisville if you need to see a doctor."

"No. It's nothing like that. I'm having lunch with a gallery owner there to discuss showing some of my art... and then afterward I'm meeting someone for coffee."

Coffee. If it was Brit, her best friend, they'd be meeting for cocktails, not coffee. "Who are you meeting for coffee?"

"It doesn't really matter, does it?" she asks. Then changing the subject, she says, "By the way, I passed by your mother's house on the way here and you might want to let Mia know that having Bennet Hayes crawling out of her bedroom window after daylight is not going to end well."

Fuck. Add it to the list. "Who are you meeting for coffee, Annalee?"

Her chin comes up. "I'm allowed to date, Clayton. Just because you didn't want me doesn't mean someone else might not!"

I knew it was coming, but I didn't expect it to cut that deep. It just sliced into me like a goddamn horror movie. "Have you seen him before?" I'm a glutton for punishment.

She sighs. "It's not like that. He works with Brit's husband, Dylan. This is just an introduction to see if we want to go out. And for the record, I didn't ask her to set me up. She wouldn't stop hounding me until I agreed to it. Happy?"

Is my fist plowing through his front teeth? "No, I'm not happy. But that doesn't really matter, does it? I'll talk to Mia."

"I didn't come here to rub that in your face...but I can't lie to you," she says softly. "I never could."

The implication is obvious. She can't lie to me, but that's clearly not a two-way street. The secrets that put us in this mess are still there, hovering between us like ghosts. "I know."

She doesn't say anything else, not because we have nothing to say to one another, but because nothing we say right now will change a damn thing. Turning, she opens the door and steps out into the dim morning light. I watch her walking to the mom-mobile that she loves to drive. It's usually filled with at least four girls and their dance gear at any given time. I don't even know this son of a bitch. He might be the nicest guy in the world, but I fucking hate him. I'd be lying if I didn't admit that I hate her a little bit right now, too.

My fist clenches, and before I can even think about what I'm doing, there's a hole in the drywall and blood on my shirt. Fuck it. I put my jacket on and head to the car. I need the distraction of work, of the distillery, of one of the things I'm trying desperately to save. Maybe it'll take the sting away from the things I've had to let go of.

ANNALEE

My hands are shaking as I drive away from Clayton's condo. I press the hands-free call button on the steering wheel and Brit picks up after only one ring.

"Tell me everything!" she squeals. "Did he plead, beg? Did he cry? I hope that son of a bitch bawled like a damn baby!"

I'm rolling my eyes, but I can't help it. I think Brit is angrier at Clayton than I'll ever be. But she doesn't see that he's hurting. I do. Maybe I shouldn't care. God knows, I've tried not to. It won't sway me. Whatever he has going on, he decided that it was more important to him than I was, and that's what I have to hold on to when I feel myself weakening.

It took me a while to get to a point of being that forgiving toward him. For the first couple of months, every time I looked at him, I wanted to claw his eyes out.

"He wasn't happy about it. I still feel like this is wrong." Brit's plan had been a little iffy for me from the start.

"Look, you want to know how he feels before it's too late, right?"

I sigh. That's the crux of it. I've yet to find whatever incentive it will take to get Clayton to just open up and tell the damn truth. We're getting a damn divorce because I banked on the fact that I meant more to him than whatever it is that he's hiding. Clearly, I was mistaken.

I'd been crying about it to Brit a few weeks ago. Her insane plan, born out of two bottles of red wine and my desperation, had unfolded. Maybe, she'd suggested, Clayton needed to be reminded that just because he didn't want me, other men wouldn't feel the same. So here I sit, having just 'inadvertently' confessed to my husband that I have a date with another man. The second part of Brit's plan was to force me to go on an actual date with someone. She said I had to, that I needed to dip my toes in the water. I was less than thrilled about that part.

"Yes," I reply. The attorneys are pouring over the final

11

settlement and custody arrangements as we speak. It is most definitely now or never.

"So get your ass here. Meet with that damn gallery owner. You've been putting your wants and your dreams on hold for long enough while you played wifey!"

That wasn't how it was. Clayton had never asked me to give up my art. He'd supported it one hundred percent. I had made that choice in a dozen little ways every day. I was the one who decided to become the dance mom, the carpooler, the cupcake baker. I'd tied myself up in every aspect of Emma Grace's life. Mostly because I was trying to be the antithesis of what my mother had been—absent. But I didn't say that to Brit. She got pissed at even a hint of me defending Clayton.

"Do I really have to go out with this guy, Brit? Can't I just cancel it?"

"You haven't looked at another man in twelve years. Not since he walked out on that balcony and looked down at you dancing around a burning couch," Brit accused. "Maybe he isn't it, Annalee? Maybe there's something out there that's better."

I don't believe that. I never have.

"Besides," she continues, "It would be a shit move to cancel on Stephen when he's going through the same thing you are. This is his first post-split foray into the dating world too."

And there it is. Guilt. No. I won't stand the poor bastard up. I'll go. We'll talk. And then I'll come home. It'll be like a two-person support group meeting.

"Fine. I'll be there. But it's just coffee and I'm telling him up front that I am not looking for anything at all."

"Fine. Do whatever. But just go. It makes it more real for you and for Clayton. You wanted to force his hand, Annalee," she reminds me. "This is the best way to do it."

"He's never been the jealous type," I protest.

"He never had to be. You looked at him like he was a god."

I have no response for that. Instead, I lie. "I'm hitting a dead spot. I'll probably lose service. I'll call you later."

I hang up the phone quickly before she can reply. It was a chicken thing to do, but I'm tired of everything being a fight. I also need to go home and get ready for my meeting with the gallery owner. I don't think there's a single thing in my wardrobe that says "serious artist." It's soccer mom, all the way.

CLAYTON

I'm walking into the office, not so quietly fuming. Based on the wide berth everyone is giving me, I'd say it's pretty obvious that I'm in a shitty mood.

I can't believe she's doing this. Our divorce isn't final. We haven't even signed the papers, and she's already moving on, dating other people. A part of me knows that I have no right to feel this way. This is all happening because of me. I did this. That doesn't make it any easier to live with. I'm dying here. Somehow, the idea of her being with another man, even if it is just an innocent meeting, that makes it feel more permanent than all the lawyers and negotiations have.

Then, there is the other issue. I'm the one who pushed Mia, who told her that if she wanted Bennett Hayes to do something about it. I also told her to be discreet, dammit. Having him crawling out of her bedroom window in the bright light of day does not fall into that description.

I climb the stairs from the distillery floor to the administrative offices. Quentin is waiting for me at the top.

"What the hell crawled up your ass?"

"I don't need your shit today, Quentin," I tell him as I brush past him.

"Wasn't aware I was giving you any," he replies. "But you look like you're on your way to commit a murder, and since I'm related to everyone who works on this floor, I figure I'm entitled to ask a question or two."

"This," I say sharply, "has nothing to do with work."

"The former ball and chain?" Quentin says, tongue in cheek.

"I'm glad you find it funny, you dick."

Quentin sighs and follows me down the hallway to my office. Of course, he would choose to be a dog with a bone today. The fuck.

Quentin is still on my heels as I retreat into my office. He drops into the chair across from my desk and then props his feet up on it like he owns the damn place. "If you want to prop your feet up and get comfy, go to your own damn office."

"I've got questions," he says. "I'm not just here to bust your balls."

"Then get to it. I'm not in the mood to be social."

Quentin continues, "We can't keep pouring money into the distillery and not getting anything back out of it. Our salaries are not even a living wage and given that you're now going to be supporting two households on it, that's gonna fucking sting."

It already stings like a damned hornet's nest. "This is not news."

"I have an investor," he says quietly.

"I'm not giving up any of our control," I remind him. "Right now, between the three of us, we can keep Samuel in check, sort of. If we let go of any of that, and this investor falls for his shit, we're fucked."

Quentin nods. "This investor would not fall for his shit because this investor is not female...second, I wasn't thinking about selling any of our shares. I was thinking about finding someone to buy out Samuel."

I'm shaking my head as I answer. "He'll never sell. Not right now. He's got the promise of the rest of Mom's inheritance coming in...as long as that little gem is hanging out there, he's got no incentive to let go of anything."

He gives me an assessing stare and I'm reminded that Quentin, partying and womanizing aside, is as shrewd as they come. "Isn't that what you're working on...finding incentive for him?"

Regardless of how shrewd he might be, and of the ruthless streak that I know he has in him, I've kept my family out of this mess for a reason and that reason has not changed. "You need to stay out of this. You and Mia. If it goes to shit, that way only of us has to take the fall," I remind him.

Quentin looks down at his folded hands. "I may have something you can use. I'll know more after this next trip to Knoxville. I've got a line on something big."

I've been digging for months and while I've found plenty of dirty secrets and shady deals, nothing concrete enough to hang the bastard. "Fine. But play it careful. No risks."

Quentin gets to his feet and straightens his suit jacket. He's always immaculately dressed, always put together. He's more vain even than Mia. "I'm always careful."

"If you see Mia," I tell him, "I need to talk to her."

He nods and exits, leaving me alone with the same miserable thoughts that were tormenting as I walked in. I can't get Annalee out of my head, her and whoever this jackass is that she's meeting. It's fucking torture.

In an effort to get my mind on work and the shit I actually need to do, I open my email and immediately wish I hadn't. The first one is from Erica. It's going to be a shit storm and I know it, but I open it anyway.

Clayton,

Given the family dynamic of the business structure at Fire Creek, I'm not in a position to lodge a formal complaint against Mia. It wouldn't do any good anyway. However, I'm putting you on notice. I'm not going to be spoken to the way she spoke to me again. The things she said are grounds for a sexual harassment suit, and if pushed, I will file it. If she continues, I will quit my job, but before I do that, I will file a complaint and I will obtain the best attorney I can to prove that she created a hostile work environment and that you, as acting CEO of Fire Creek, supported it. Not to mention, I'll be only too happy to relay that information to your father. I don't think he'd be pleased.

Erica.

Fuck me. Running my hands through my hair in frustration, I consider how to proceed. I can't respond to it immediately. I can't. Whatever I say would be evidence, and I'm not in any frame of mind to deal with her shit.

The next email is no better. It's from a friend of mine at the bank who has been monitoring our father's spending and alerting me, against every rule in the book, of any major purchases or suspicious activity. The son of a bitch has rented a condo in Los Cabos for a weekend. And Erica hasn't asked for any time off, so clearly, she won't be accompanying him. No wonder she's threatening to sue over Mia's little tirade the other day. Erica is no dummy. She sees the writing on the wall and knows that her tenure with Samuel is just about up. Her expiration date is on the horizon.

I'm interrupted from considering the dire ramifications of a lawsuit when there's a knock at the door. I call out for the person to enter but my tone is definitely less than welcoming.

"I take it you're having a bad morning?" Mia asks walking into the office.

"You might say that. Dad has been shopping again."

"Shopping for what?" she asks, settling into the chair that Quentin so recently vacated.

"Women. Erica is in an uproar, threatening to quit... the problem with that is she knows all about this company. She knows about the massive auction of our product in Japan."

"So she has the power to sink us, and now she has the motivation to do so," Mia states it matter-of-factly, without emotion.

"That's about it. So, don't piss her off any more than necessary, okay? I can't put out any more fires today."

"What other fires have you had to put out?" she asked.

I look up at her, but I'm not answering questions. She doesn't need to know about Annalee and she sure as hell doesn't need to know about whatever mystery Quentin is working on. "Nothing important," I reply, shutting down further questions. "I've got work to do, and so do you. If you want to look into working with Keeneland, I need that proposal by the end of the day...

and Mia, make damn sure that Bennett Hayes climbs down that tree outside your window before daylight next time, okay?"

She blinks at me in surprise. Like I wouldn't find out in a town the size of Fontaine. "Excuse me?"

"Annalee came by this morning and asked me to pick up the munchkin from school this afternoon because she's got to go to Louisville."

"What's she going to Louisville for?"

I can feel my expression hardening. But I'm not about to discuss that topic any more than necessary. I don't want the pity that would result. "I'm not her husband anymore. I don't get to ask those kinds of questions. Point being, she saw him shimmying down that damn oak tree...do what you want, but for the love of God, be discreet."

Mia puts her hands on her hips and glares at me the same way she did when she was four. It's considerably less adorable now. "Were you, or were you not, the one who told me to go for it?"

"Yes. Go for it. Enjoy it. You deserve this and a hell of a lot more, but be smart about it. Samuel gets wind of this and everything I—" I stop abruptly. I've made it a point to keep my investigation of Samuel a secret. Sure, they know I'm doing it, but no one knows what I've found and I need to keep it that way until I've got the smoking gun in my possession.

"Everything what? Clayton, just tell me what you're doing. You've been keeping secrets and I know they're about him and it's costing you everything. Tell me and I will help you."

"I can't," I say. "The things I'm working on, Mia, they're not really above board. I'm not cutting corners with the business. I would *never* do that. But to get what I need on him, to get the upper hand that I have to have to make this work, I can't play by the rules. And I won't let anyone else take those risks."

"What things are you working on? Clayton, for the love of all that's holy, just tell me! You're keeping all those secrets and it's going to be the death of you."

My hands are in my hair again, this time pressing at my temples where the headache is building from a dull roar to an agonizing scream. "As much of a shit as Samuel's been to us, fucking people over isn't restricted to family. I'm digging, Mia, digging up every bit of dirt and filth on him I can...you can't do that without getting a little dirty yourself."

"What have you done?" There's fear in her voice, worry for me and for everyone else.

"Nothing that I can't come back from. Not yet, anyway," I tell her. It isn't completely true, but if it will ease her mind, so be it.

"This isn't good for you." There are tears in her eyes. Mia, in spite of her stoic resolve and her usually calm demeanor, is a softie on the inside. She's got a tender heart. I know, because I watched our father break it.

"No, but he isn't good for anyone. And if I can build a life here, for all of us, that he doesn't get to taint with his presence, it's worth the cost...so just be smart. Be discreet. And let me handle Samuel when the time comes."

Mia doesn't say anything else. She just stands there looking at me quietly for a moment before turning and heading out the door, presumably to her own office.

The rest of the day goes by in a blur. I finish up payroll, handle some complaints from distributors because they don't have the product they need.

Bourbon production cannot be rushed. The four-year mark is a guideline, not a hard and fast date. The barrels aren't ready yet. Maybe another month, maybe another four, but I can't say. It's simply done when it's done, and if they don't want to wait for it, then we'll just find new distributors.

I leave the office and drive to the elementary school to wait in the purgatory that is the pick-up line. There's another car beside me, and I know the woman behind the wheel. She's recently divorced and I can feel her eyes on me while I sit there, trapped.

She rolls down her window. "Clayton Darcy, is that you?"

Fuck. I roll down my own window. "Hello, Gina. How are you?"

She smiles flirtatiously. "You ought to come over sometime and I'll show you."

That is never going to happen. "It was good talking to you, Gina. I'd prefer to keep our conversation and our interactions G-rated, if possible."

She huffs out a breath, clearly insulted. "It's your loss."

"I'm sure it is. Have a good evening." And that is why I hate to pick up Emma Grace at school. Every single, almost single, and unhappily married woman in Fontaine is looking at me like a fat kid looks at cake. I'm not stupid enough to think it's because I'm that hot. In this town, the name Darcy equals money, at least to people who don't realize we're all teetering on the edge of bankruptcy. And since Annalee cut me loose, they're looking at me as a reasonably attractive meal ticket.

The line moves steadily forward. I'm close enough to the front door now that I can see Emma Grace. My heart melts. That's the only way to describe it. Every time I look at her, it just gets me. She's wearing a pink dress and a white sweater and the ugliest fucking cowboy boots I've ever seen.

I can picture her and Annalee fighting over those boots in the morning. Emma Grace usually wins out just by sheer force of will and the overwhelming use of the word *why*. People underestimate the power of the word until they're dealing with a stubborn child. Then it takes on a whole new meaning.

She runs forward, ignoring the teachers telling her not to, and opens the car door.

"Daddy, I don't like boys," she says as she climbs into the back seat and buckles herself in.

"Boys in general, or a boy in particular?" I don't really care. I just pray for a few more years of reprieve. The thought of some god-awful, horny ass, disgusting teenage boy ever looking at her makes me want to increase the size of my gun collection.

"Most boys. Some are okay. But Cody Blevins picked his nose...and then..." She pauses for dramatic effect. "He *ate* it, Daddy. He's soooo gross."

I'm laughing as I finally escape the school parking lot. "That is pretty gross, baby," I agree. Really that's all I have to do with Emma Grace. She tells me about her day, I agree as needed. If only all relationships with women could be so simple.

"I'm hungry," she announces.

"Pizza?"

She's dancing in the back seat now. Pizza is always a winner. I turn the car toward Main Street and the only pizza place in town. It's been there forever. Hell, I used to hang out there in high school.

When we arrive, Annalee makes a beeline for the ancient Pac-Man machine and I grab one of the cracked vinyl booths where I can keep my eye on her. She's the only thing keeping me sane right now. In all the rest of the craziness, I know that when she sees me, her face will light

21

up. There's no anger or disappointment there. Did any of us ever look at Samuel that way?

I don't think so. Even searching my childhood memories, all I can recall is the sense of dread, of knowing that when he walked in, whatever we were doing wouldn't be good enough, would be messy, or sloppy and reflecting poorly on the Darcy family name.

"Daddy, can I have some quarters?"

I dig in my pocket for change and give her the few quarters that are in the mix.

I want this back. Not weekends. Not random nights when Annalee is sitting in a bar having martinis with some asshole I don't even know. I want us. Me, her and Emma Grace coming to this shithole for pizza on the weekend, or driving up to Newport to the Aquarium.

I see Emma Grace's face fall as she fails epically at Pac-Man. It's a common occurrence. When the last of her quarters are gone, she comes back to the table just as the waitress is there to get our order.

"Pepperoni?"

"And extra cheese," she says, grinning for added effect.

"And extra cheese," I agree. "Water to drink."

"I want a pop."

"Your mother doesn't let you have pop," I reply. She's tried this before, seeing if I'll bend the rules. "It rots your teeth and then I'll be in trouble."

She makes a face, but doesn't say anything. Emma Grace is the one thing that Annalee and I have done completely right. She's a good kid—even with the mess our lives are in, she's a happy kid.

"So what happened at school besides that kid eating boogers?" I ask her.

She wrinkles up her nose and looks so much like

Annalee, it's a punch in the gut. "Allison told me her parents are getting a divorce like you and Mom."

Do eight-year-olds really sit around talking about divorce? What the hell? "Is she okay with that?" Are you? I'm afraid to ask that question.

"I don't think so," she replies, twirling a straw on the table. "But she said her daddy moved in with his girlfriend. Are you going to do that?"

"No. I'm not moving in with anyone else." If I can't have Annalee, there's no one else I want.

"I want you to come back home." Her expression is so serious, so solemn that it's just fucking torture. This may be the only time in my life that I can't give my daughter what she wants.

I shake my head. "It's not that easy. Your mom is really mad at me...and she has a good reason to be."

"Tell her you're sorry and you won't do it again." She offers that sage bit of advice with complete conviction.

"I'll try that. It might not work for me the way it does for you...I think you need pigtails for it to be truly effective." I reach out and tug one of her braids to make the point. It has the desired effect and sets her giggling. That's the sound I want to hear. No more talk about divorces and people's parents moving out. She shouldn't have to think about these things.

ANNALEE

I'm sitting at a bar that I don't want to be in, listening to a man that I absolutely despise. Somehow the coffee date had switched to cocktails and I'm actually grateful. I need the dulling effect of alcohol.

This is not a two-person support group. It's a one man show. We've talked about his work, his house, his boat. We've talked about his ex, his workout regimen, which incidentally is puny. I could kick his ass three ways from Sunday in the gym. But the bottom line is, we haven't talked. He has talked. And I have sipped way more of my wine than I meant to, because I haven't been able to get a word in edgewise.

"You know you're much prettier than I expected," he says, and the way he smiles at me makes my skin crawl a little. Is this seriously who my friends see me with? Have I pissed Brit off without knowing it?

"That's nice," I respond lamely. "Thanks, I think."

He clearly doesn't get that my response wasn't genuine flattery as he's now resting his slightly sweaty hand on my knee. "You know, Annalee, we could go back to my place. Kick back and relax on the couch, maybe watch a movie?"

No, sir. There will be no Netflix and chill. What the ever-loving fuck is wrong with men? Are they all this damn dumb?

"I've really enjoyed meeting you, Steve, but I need to be going now." At great personal cost, I force myself to be polite, to say something other than take your paws off me, you reptilian scumbag.

"Are you sure you have to go? It's still early," he says, and checks his very expensive watch for the umpteenth time that evening. Yes. I saw your Omega. Yes. I get that it's super expensive and means you're loaded with credit card debt. No. I'm not impressed. All this asshole has done is make me miss Clayton, which in turn makes me even madder at Clayton. I wouldn't be here putting up with this self-important dick if my almost-ex-husband weren't such a high handed, know it all asshole!

"It is early," I agree. "But I'm ready to go home... alone. Have a nice evening."

Apparently, he's not completely obtuse. Just mostly. He picks up on the unimpressed tone and the clear lack of infatuation with him that time. He sneers at me. "It's no damn wonder your husband left you."

"He didn't leave. I threw him out...but on that same note, if I'd been married to you, I would have cheated. I would *so* have cheated. The fact that your wife stayed faithful for seven years should get her nominated for sainthood." I pick up my wineglass and drain the rest of it. "Thanks for the drink and the reminder that my ex isn't so bad after all."

I march out to my car, leaving several people snickering in my wake. I'm too drunk to drive and if I take a cab to Brit's house, I'll spend the rest of the night getting the third degree on why I didn't like him, and how impossibly high my standards are. Or worse, she'll tell me the truth, that I came on this date wanting to hate him because he's not Clayton. Well, to hell with that. I'll just sit in my car and sober up.

I pull my phone out of my purse and open the reading app on it. There's a smutty novel I've been meaning to get to and there's no time like the present.

Two

CLAYTON

I got Emma Grace off to school. Her socks don't match, but in those cowboy boots, no one will know. Her ponytail might also be a little less than perfect. I'm not like Annalee who will fight with her over her hair. She says it hurts and I say that tangle can stay there until her mother wants to remove it.

"Get your backpack," I tell her as I grab one of the Pop-Tarts from the toaster. "And don't tell your mother that breakfast involved frosting."

With her pink backpack hanging off her shoulder, she takes the Pop-Tart with a grin. "And sprinkles."

"Secret, Emma Grace. Pinky swear?"

She holds out her tiny hand and we lock pinkies for a second. "You've got all your stuff for dance practice after school?" I ask.

I run a damn distillery and the kid has more appointments to keep track of than I do.

"Yes," she replies with an eye roll. "Miss Lisa says I can try out for the Nutcracker this year."

Of course Miss Lisa told her that. Miss Lisa is all about anything that will help her draw more students to her ballet school which costs the damn earth. "We'll see. Let's go, munchkin. We've both got work to do."

I drop Emma Grace off at school. She waves to me from the door and then I head to the distillery. Once I'm in the office, I'm looking at the mountain of paperwork on my desk, but all I can think about is my wife going out with another man. She really did it. She went on a date. I know because she called Emma Grace before bed last night to tell her good night. I could hear it in her voice that she was just a little buzzed on wine.

Did she kiss him? Is she going to see him again? Did she go home with him? Those questions won't stop and they're making me crazy. I never thought it would go this far. I thought, before final papers were drawn up and settlements were reached, that I would have this nightmare with Samuel done and over with and I could explain it all to her. I could win her back.

It hurt me to leave, it fucking gutted me to walk out of that house and leave her alone. But I never felt, until this very moment, that I was really losing her forever.

Quentin rolls into the office and he looks like hell. He's wearing jeans and a sweater rather than his usual suit, he hasn't shaved and he smells like a brewery.

"Where the hell have you been?" I demand.

He plops down across from my desk and puts his feet up in a repeat of yesterday's performance. But he's got a wide, shit-eating grin on his face. "Is that any way to greet the man who saved the motherfucking day?"

This should be good. "Lay it on me."

"I met someone in a bar a couple of weeks ago who

told me that Samuel sold his boat because he was trying to hide evidence."

"Evidence of what?" I ask.

Quentin takes his feet off the desk and leans forward, resting his elbows on his knees. "That he was with Katherine Shelby the day she drowned."

Okay. That's bigger than I expected. Katherine Shelby was a party girl, a beautiful debutante a year younger than Quentin. But in her late twenties, she'd developed an affinity for older, wealthier men. We've never been able to link them, never been able to find any proof other than a single overheard phone conversation that would never hold up. "Do you really think he killed her?"

"Do you really question whether or not he's capable of it?" Quentin fires back.

No. Not in the least. But I do question whether or not Samuel would ever sully his own hands with it. "Is there any proof?"

"I have the name and address of a witness. I'll be back with all the proof we need," he promises.

"Quentin, people don't speak out against Samuel. Even when they want to. We both know that," I remind him. He plays dirty, lying, blackmailing, threats...whatever it takes, Samuel covers his tracks and keeps witnesses in line.

"I can be pretty damn persuasive." Quentin gets to his feet. "I have to go out of town for a week or so. The witness is down in Knoxville. It might take a little a time to coax them into offering up what we need."

"You mean coax her," I correct him.

"Whatever it takes."

I worry about Quentin. In his own way, I think he might be the most miserable of us all. He was always so close to our mother. Her accident left him lost, for lack of a better word. And even though he finished school and appears to be functional, I know there's something broken inside him because of it. "Be careful, Quent. I want the bastard to burn, but not at the cost of your soul. He's not worth it."

"That's a little pot and kettle, don't you think?"

It is. But I'm already screwed. I watch Quentin walk out. Part of me hopes he gets what we need and another part of me hopes it's a dead end. I don't want him to have to live with any more regret.

By the time I'm done with the mountain of paperwork, the phone calls, and trying to figure out how to stretch my meager savings and even slimmer salary to cover my rent and the mortgage for the next few months, it's nearly dark outside. Annalee has already picked up Emma Grace, gotten her from school to dance practice and home again. And I'm still sitting at the damn distillery, alone in the dark.

Sounds about right.

My phone dings and I glance at the screen. I leave everything behind and head out. I don't know what the hell is going on, but it can't possibly be good.

The only thing worse than a pissed off wife is a pissed off almost ex-wife. So when you get a cryptic text message from one telling you to bring your ass home; you, by God, bring your ass *home*. I have no idea what the hell is going on, only that hell might have frozen over or Jesus might have come again. Of course, there's a memory trying desperately to rear its ugly head, along with other things, of a time when Annalee texted me to get my ass home and met me at the door completely naked except for hooker red lipstick. Pretty safe to say I won't be getting that welcome again anytime soon.

Parking my car in the driveway, I feel like a damn guest. Every fucking time I come here I feel that way. My soon-to-be ex-wife knows that. It's like a twisting knife in the gut when I ring the doorbell and stand there waiting for her to send Emma Grace out to me. I haven't been permitted back inside since the night I left. I'll give her one thing, she knows how to tip the balance of power in her direction and keep it that way.

Most of the time, it's not so bad. Until the other day when she dropped the bomb about her date, we'd hit a stride where we could converse politely with one another, like strangers, like we didn't share a bed for nearly twelve years, like I haven't tasted every inch of her body, like we didn't have a child together. We're like polite yet respect-fully distant neighbors now. It's almost worse that way, especially since I can't get out of my head the vision of her with some faceless stranger. Somehow, it was better when she was calling me every kind of son of a bitch to ever walk. At least then, as long as she was still angry at me, I felt like it wasn't really over.

I march up to the door. It might not be my house anymore, but I'm still paying the mortgage and I'll be damned if I ring the fucking doorbell like a Jehovah's Witness. Instead, I raise my fist and knock with a little more force than is necessary.

I hear a scream from inside the house. I pound on the door again. "Annalee?"

There's nothing. I bang on the door again. "Annalee, if you don't answer me, I'm breaking the damn door down!"

Footsteps are approaching at a run, which does

nothing to ease my fear. When Annalee yanks the door open, her eyes are wild, and she's clearly in a panic. She reaches out, grabs hold of my tie, and pulls me inside.

"I'm so glad you're here!" she gushes. It's been a long time since she sounded that happy to see me.

"If you're so glad to see me, try not to choke me to death," I tell her as I tug the fabric from her fingers. "What the hell is going on?"

She glances back at me over her shoulder as she grasps my hand. It's the first time she's touched me willingly in six months. She tugs me toward the kitchen. "I don't have the words...you just have to see it. The sink—exploded!" She stops abruptly, her face crumples and I can see the tears beginning. That's how I know it's bad. My Annalee is a lot of things, but she's not a crier. *She's not yours anymore.* That voice whispering in my head, reminding me of the very painful truth, sounds a lot like the man I blame for it. Samuel Darcy.

We round the corner and with the sight that greets me, I completely understand her urgency. The faucet from the sink is just gone and in its place is a fountain. A geyser of water is spraying upward, showering everything, and more of it is pouring out from beneath the sink. The kitchen floor is completely flooded and the whole goddamn place is a mess.

"Where's my toolbox?" I ask. "Is it still in the garage?"

She spares me a glance that clearly indicates I am too stupid to live. "Where the hell else would it be?"

In no mood for attitude from anyone, but especially her at the moment, I snap back. "At Goodwill with the rest of my shit?"

She has the grace to blush at that and I know that's as close to an apology or admission of guilt as she'll come.

"Get my toolbox," I tell her again as I wade through

the several inches of water that are forming a pool in the kitchen and making a waterfall out of the steps down into the garage.

Reaching under the cabinet, I find the shut-off valve but the damn thing is stuck. Taking a kitchen towel from the drawer, I try again. No luck. I twist the towel around the valve and then insert the handle of a wooden spoon from the jar on the counter. Twisting the towel with the spoon, I finally get it tight enough to get the torque I need to get the valve to budge.

After what seems like forever, the valve finally gives, turning slowly in the right direction. The water slows to a trickle and finally shuts off altogether, just as Annalee walks in carrying my toolbox.

"What the hell happened here?" I knew the minute I asked the question that it was the wrong thing to do. My tone was too sharp, my attitude a little too proprietorial. Her shoulders tense and square, her chin juts out like she's ready for a fight, and I can see the daggers in her eyes from across the room. I'm fucked and not in the good way.

"I didn't do this, Clayton!" Her voice was a low, angry hiss, the same one she'd used when she'd all but handed me my suitcase and told me to get the hell out.

"I never said you did, Annalee...I think my exact words were what happened...not what did you do. Can we skip the fight already? I'll apologize now, you can tell me what a son of a bitch I am and then we can get down to the business of figuring out how not to have to replace the wood floors and half the cabinets."

"*You* don't have to do anything! It's my house. My responsibility!" she retorts.

"*You*," I snap back at her, "don't have to have a job!"

"I'm selling art! A lot of it, actually."

"Enough to pay the mortgage?" I ask.

She clams up then. I can see the reluctance to answer in her eyes. Finally, she offers a grudging, "No."

I walk out to the garage and grab the giant squeegee we use for the windows and open the garage door. Might as well let gravity work in our favor and get rid of most of the water that way. Annalee grabs a large broom and we both head back into the kitchen and start forcing the standing water toward the door and down the steps into the garage where it can drain naturally down the slight slope of the driveway.

By the time we're done, I'm sweating even though my clothes are still soaked with icy water. I lug the Shop-Vac up the steps and Annalee goes to work, getting up the rest of the water while I set up fans to help with air flow. We had worked almost silently, I realize. We'd fallen into a rhythm like we used to whenever we were doing a project together. I'd almost forgotten how well we work together.

When the task is done, the kitchen drying, I look back at her and immediately wish I hadn't.

Her cheeks are flushed, she's breathing hard, and then I realize that the T-shirt she's wearing is almost completely transparent from the water. It's not like I haven't seen her tits before. I'm damn well acquainted with them. That's the problem. I'm not just looking at them. I'm remembering how they feel, the taste of her skin, the sounds she makes when I apply just the right amount of pressure with my teeth. Son of a bitch.

"Stop looking at me like that," she says.

"Can't help it. I'm hardwired to look at boobs...even those I've seen before," I reply.

"You're such an asshole, Clay."

There isn't any heat behind it. She's just speaking matter-of-factly. But honestly, in this moment, I don't care. All the blood in my body is rushing south, straight to my cock. I can't think of anything but her. Wet. Naked. Grinding against me and begging for more.

I know the moment her mind goes to the same place I can't get mine to leave. I see her pupils dilate, her lips part. The tension between us is a living, breathing thing. But I know, there's no good way for this to end. We're either sexually frustrated or filled with regret.

To break the tension, I say, "Emma Grace will be so upset that she missed a chance to swim in the kitchen."

The pitiful attempt at humor did its job. There's a smile playing at her lips. She won't let it out, but I know it's there. She gestures toward the sink. "Yes, she will. If she'd been here, she would have had on flippers and goggles before we could even turn around...I don't know what you just did, but I've never been so happy to see you in my life."

I can't help but grin. "This trumps our first date, our wedding and the birth of our child? Really?"

"Well, not trumps," she admits reluctantly. "But this was pretty high on my disaster list...They were working on the water line down the street today. It was shut off for hours. And I guess I didn't have the taps off, after all. When they turned the water back on, all the air pressure in the pipes—it's just a disaster."

I can't remember the last time we talked when it wasn't about Emma Grace's schedule or this paper or that paper needing to be signed and delivered to the attorneys. Somewhere along the way, in the process of being parents and homeowners and running businesses, we forgot how to be a couple. That doesn't just get laid at my door either. Long before Japan, long before I found out the truth of what Samuel was, and what I'd have to do to free us all from him, we'd been drifting apart. We're both guilty. All I know is that right now, I feel closer to her than I have in more than a year, and it's not enough. Not even close.

ANNALEE

I can feel his gaze on me, the weight of it is substantial, almost like he's touching me. I know I'm a mess. My hair is tied up in a ponytail and the truth is that I can't even remember if I brushed it today. I'm wearing one of his T-shirts and praying to God he doesn't notice and comment. Either way, it's soaking wet and completely see through, so if he's looking at what the shirt says and not my boobs, then divorce was definitely the right move.

His eyes begin to wander, moving from my face to my chest then down, and slowly, very slowly back up. I know that look. I've seen it on his face more times than I can count. I respond to it accordingly, like I've been conditioned to it. My nipples grow hard, aching beneath the damp fabric and I can feel myself getting wet for him. I hate that he still has the power to do that to me without even touching me.

"I know what you're thinking," I tell him. "And you can just stop. That isn't going to happen. Never again."

He doesn't smile at me. But his eyes crinkle at the corner the way they always do before he unleashes that devastatingly sexy grin that just makes my panties fall off. It doesn't help that we christened every room in this house and that while standing in this kitchen all I can think about is the time he fucked me against the refrigerator hard enough that we actually broke the damned ice maker. Afterward, he just smiled and said it was worth it.

"Just remembering the good times," he replies. "There were a lot of them."

"There were a lot of bad too," I point out. I hate being a bitch to him. It just sneaks out. The simple truth of it is that I never intended to divorce Clayton. I was stupid enough to think that when I gave him that ultimatum, that he had to tell me what the hell he was hiding or we were done, I really believed I was important enough to him that he'd do what I asked. Even with Brit's idiotic plan of me going out on a date, which was a disaster of epic proportion, he hadn't reacted the way I'd expected.

For the last year, things had been wrong with us. Since Clayton and his brother and sister bought into the distillery and took over the running of it from Samuel, things had just been off with us. After his trip to Japan, he wouldn't even look at me or touch me. I thought at first it was an affair, but I know him. I know that's not who he is. Or at least I thought I knew him. When I asked for a divorce and his only response was "okay" that was a little unexpected.

Now he's standing in this kitchen looking at me like he could sop me up with a biscuit. I want to be pissed. I want so badly to just tear into him and let him have it, but all I can think about is getting naked and rolling around with him on a flooded kitchen floor.

If my wet clothes are a problem, his aren't helping. His white dress shirt is plastered to his chest. Why the hell do men just look sexier with their cuffs rolled back?

"You think we can focus on the kitchen for the moment?" *Something that's fixable.*

"It's not that much of a disaster," he says, finally dragging his eyes off me and the T-shirt that's practically pornographic at the moment. "Once it dries, we'll figure out how much damage is done to the floor. We need to open all the cabinet doors though, get some air flowing and maybe empty out the bottom ones."

And there he is. The man I married. The decision maker. The I-can-fix-this man. Every problem we ever had, every issue that ever came up, he always had a plan. And until a year ago, he always shared it with me.

"You don't have to do that. You don't live here anymore. It's not your responsibility." The minute the words are out, I know I've made an awful mistake. Any hint of teasing is gone from his face. He's pissed, and not just a little.

"Why don't you just take the fucking knives from the drawer and stab me?" he asks. "It'd be kinder."

"I didn't mean it that way," I offer. "Really."

"And I didn't offer because it was my responsibility. I'm here. It's no trouble," he says and starts opening up cabinet drawers and pulling out all the cast iron cookware that I'd collected needlessly.

I watch the play of muscle under the wet cotton of his shirt as he lugs everything toward the counter. Everything about him looks good, and it's killing me. "I'm sorry. I shouldn't have asked you to come...but I couldn't get the water to shut off, and it just kept pouring out and—I'm sorry, Clayton. I just didn't know what else to do."

"It's fine. I don't mind helping out," he replies. "I know I don't live here, Annalee. And maybe it won't be true for much longer, but right now, I'm still your husband."

Yes. He is. And it's killing me. I change the subject. "I must have scared you to death with that text," I continue, striving for a tone of normalcy, as if I'm not standing there torn between railing at him and ripping both our clothes off. "I didn't think about how it sounded at the time! I was just so frantic. You're a saint for coming so quickly."

"I needed to talk to you anyway...about helping out with Mama. I know it's a lot to ask, but—"

I shake my head immediately. This is not a question that even needs to be asked. "I'll help with Patricia as long as you need me to. You know that! She's Emma's grandmother, for goodness' sake."

He shoves his hands in his pockets and leans back against the counter. He's wearing his thinking expression and then, decision made, he opens his mouth and starts to speak. "Mia is still seeing Bennett Hayes. I expect it all to get ugly soon."

I don't know his stance on the issue. He was pissed enough when I'd told him about seeing Bennett climbing down from Mia's window while driving Emma Grace to school one morning. But that is a touchy subject for a lot of people. "Are you going to intervene?" I ask.

He smirks. "I already have. I was the one who told Bennett that if he wanted her, he needed to do something about it...they're not kids anymore."

That was so not what I expected. "You—what the hell, Clayton?"

He shrugs in response, the movement emphasizing the breadth of his shoulders. I realize he looks even better than he did when we first met twelve years ago. There are just a few strands of silver in his brown hair, and his features have hardened, become more masculine and rugged rather than just being pretty the way he was as a younger man. He walks over to where I'm standing and removes his loosened necktie, tugging it from his collar in a move that is so dead sexy I have to clench my thighs together.

"The night of Mia's accident, he came back to see her...and it just hit me that there really isn't any reason for them to be apart unless that's what they want." He explains it clearly, and while I know he's talking about them, the look in his eyes, the way he's staring at me, tells me he's also talking about us. I squash that little bit of hope. It's pointless, I remind myself. He made a choice, and it wasn't me.

"How'd that go over?" I ask, trying to keep the conversation focused on them, on anything but us.

Clayton laughs, really laughs in a way that I haven't seen in so long it hurts me to think about it. "Before or after he told me to go fuck myself?"

I gasp, not because Bennett said it, but because Clayton doesn't seem to mind it. "Did he really?"

"Thereabouts," he admits, a grin curving his lips that makes my heart race. "Not that I blame him. The last time he came after my sister, I did beat the shit out of him...but I didn't have a choice."

I know the story. Clayton wasn't a violent person. He could be when pushed, but he'd never been one to fight just for the hell of it. That was Quentin. Mad at the world and looking for a place to put it. But he'd beaten the hell out of Bennett the night he and Mia had been supposed to elope.

If he hadn't, Samuel would have killed Bennett. It had nothing to do with Mia, nothing to do with protecting his daughter. Bennett's only crime was having the last name of Hayes. Samuel hated him out of habit, out of spite, and out of pride.

"You're a good big brother to her," I tell him. "And you're a good father. I give you shit a lot...more than I ought to because—I just didn't see us here, Clay. I didn't see us in this spot. But whatever it is, you're a good man."

His eyes darken, fill with shadows of things I just don't understand. "I'm not," he says. "I used to think

39

that, but...I'm Samuel Darcy's son. I can't get away from that."

I don't know what this about. I'm afraid to know. Clayton has always been sure, confident. Steady and rock-solid. This man, with the darkness in his eyes and the banked fury I can sense in him, I don't know this man.

Changing the subject, I say, "Mia is happy, I think. As happy as she'll let herself be."

He nods. "I don't know who long it'll last. Even if it's not forever, it's better than nothing, right?" His expression changes, shifts into something dark for a moment, then fades again.

He walks toward me and I can't catch my breath. I know that look on his face, the tension in his jaw and the fire burning in his eyes. I've seen it more times than I can count. He stops just a few inches from me. "Are you happy?"

No. I'm lonely. I miss you. I miss the way we used to be. I miss having you hold me and I miss being the one who could make you laugh. "I have a good life." The non-answer rolls off my tongue easily enough. "I know how hard you've worked, Clayton, to give me this...to stay home with our daughter, to keep this house for her. I will always be grateful for that."

His jaw clenches, and I can see that underneath the desire still burning, there's anger and hurt. I can't understand why. He chose to leave, he chose to keep his secrets instead of sharing them with me.

"I didn't ask if you were grateful. I asked if you were happy," he growls. "Did my moving out, leaving you alone here with Emma Grace, make you happy?"

"We shouldn't do this." The protest is weak. A part of me wants to do it. A part of me wants to hash out everything, to lay out all our secrets and all our dirty laundry once and for all.

"Why not? It's about damn time we said things that matter! I'm tired, Annalee!" As he speaks, his hands move up to my shoulders, his fingers dig into the tense muscles there, pressing in with that intense mixture of pleasure and pain that just turns my body to jello.

"Tired of what?" I ask the question striving to sound normal, to sound like I don't want to just rip his clothes off and rub my naked body against his.

"Of pretending," he says softly, and he leans in close enough that his breath is moving over the skin of my neck, waking nerve endings and impulses that have been dormant for so long. "Fuck being polite. Fuck being an adult. How about let's just be honest?" he asks.

"No," I admit in a whisper so broken it's barely audible. "I'm not happy. I wasn't happy before you left and I'm not any happier now. But I got tired, Clayton! I got tired of trying to fix what was broken between us when I couldn't even get you to look at me!"

"I'm looking at you right now," he insists, and his hands move from my shoulders up to my hair, dislodging my haphazard ponytail and threading through my hair. He's not gentle, but I don't want him to be. When he tightens his hand, tugging at my hair, tilting my head back, my whole body reacts. My nipples harden instantly and I can feel the rush of heat between my thighs, that empty, aching feeling that will only be satisfied by him.

Even wanting him as I do, I know this isn't a smart move. "You do realize what a disastrous mistake we're making right now, don't you?" I'm just poking at him now, pissing him off because I can. I don't even understand it myself. There's a well of pettiness inside me that I'm truly shocked at.

"Like that's new," he snaps. "Disastrous mistakes are kinda our thing."

I don't reply. It isn't really an option. His hands have tightened in my hair again, tugging my head back. I don't even have time to formulate a response before his mouth is on mine. Hot, hungry, demanding. It's a voracious kiss, consuming, needy, demanding, even a little rough. It's all teeth and clashing tongues. And I want him so fucking bad I could die from it.

It's all here, I realize. The anger, the need, the hurt, the bitter loneliness and all the pent-up frustration of the last year are being poured into this kiss. My arms close around him of their own volition, tugging him closer until we're plastered to one another, impossible to tell where one body ends and another begins. It's still not close enough. It'll never be close enough.

My hands roam over his shoulders, over impressively bulging biceps, and then down to his hips. Clinging to him, I press my own hips forward, heightening the intimacy. I can feel him through the damp fabric of our clothes—hot, hard, urgent. I don't want him to make love to me. I don't want him to be sweet and tender. I just want him to fuck me so hard I can't think.

I am on the verge of making a huge mistake, of fucking my almost ex-husband in what was formerly *our* kitchen. He moves his hips, grinding against me, hitting a spot that makes me see stars. I don't care if it's a mistake.

I grab the front of his shirt, ripping it open, buttons scatter over the wet floor. He shivers against me and it feels like a victory. But Clayton turns the tables almost instantly. He grabs my hips, his fingers digging into my skin and pulls me toward the edge of the counter.

The hard length of him presses against me, but it still

isn't enough. The need to feel him inside me, to have him take me, is overwhelming.

His hands snake beneath my shirt, dragging the fabric up and then over my head. He closes his hands over my breasts before the discarded garment even hits the counter behind me. The sensation of his rough callused hands kneading my flesh, of his long, skilled fingers strumming my nipples to taut peaks, has me rocking against him, pressing my hips more firmly against his.

God above, his hands. He knows just how to touch me, but then he always did.

The ringing of his phone breaks the spell. It had just been the two of us, but now the world is intruding, pulling him away from me...again. "Don't answer it." I'm ashamed of how I sound, pleading and desperate.

He pulls back from me, takes his phone from his pocket, and looks at the screen. "It's Mia," he says. "She wouldn't be calling if it weren't important."

The fact that it's true doesn't make it any easier to tolerate. Pressing my hands to the edge of the counter, I shifted backward enough to sit up without landing on the floor and watch as he drifts away from me all over again.

Three

CLAYTON

I try to rein it in, but Annalee has me so wound up it's all I can do to form coherent sentences. It's a damned awkward thing to be standing there with a raging erection, a half naked woman in front of you and your damn sister on the phone. Pressing the button to accept the call, I bark into the phone, "What?"

From the other end of the line, Mia's voice sounds strained. "I'm not coming to work tomorrow."

She cock blocked me to play hooky from work. "Why the hell are you calling me about this?" I demand.

"Don't fucking take that tone with me, Clayton," she snaps back. "I've had a hell of a night and I'm sitting here with a gun in my hand."

That got my attention. It cut through everything else, including the lust induced fog, and panic took over. I talk to her calmly, pleadingly, like I would a small child. "Mia, don't do anything stupid—"

"I'm more apt to be homicidal than suicidal, you jackass."

I can't stop the sigh of relief at her smart-ass response. That's the Mia I know. She gives more shit than she takes, always, except where our father is concerned. I don't understand the power he has over her. It sure as hell isn't love. She hates him more than I do, and that says a damned lot. "Why do you have the gun?" I'm trying to focus on the important stuff, but my brain still isn't fully functional. Annalee's eyes widen in shock and she gapes at me as the conversation goes off the deep end.

I reach out, grasping her hand, holding it in mine. It isn't about the heat or the need of a few moments ago. It's about the fact that my family, my whole goddamn life is spiraling out of control. I need the contact with her, and for now, she's allowing it.

"Because I came home and thought someone had broken in. Turns out the new caregiver I hired for Mama was snooping through the house looking for old love letters."

She's losing me again, shifting gears too quickly. "I'm not following."

"What's going on?" Annalee asks in a whisper. I shake my head at her. I have no idea what the hell is going on... still.

Naturally, Mia picks up on the female voice in the background. "Who's there with you?" she demands.

"I'm not at home," I answer. I don't want to discuss what almost happened with Annalee and myself with anyone other than her.

"Oh, you're at home. Just not your home, although, since you're still paying the mortgage on it, I guess that's up for debate...I'm having the worst fucking night of my life and you're screwing your soon-to-be ex-wife?"

"That is not what's going on here," I protest. It is, but I'm sure as hell not doing to discuss that with my sister. I don't know what's going on with Mia. She sounds wild, a little crazed, and angrier than I've ever heard her. "Mia, you've got to calm down." Annalee, halfway through the process of putting her shirt back on, is making cutting motions across her throat and rolling her eyes at me. I made the fatal error of telling a woman to calm down. It's all a clusterfuck.

"No, I don't! I've been calm. I've been quiet. I've done what the dutiful daughter ought to and I've spent ten years making up for something I didn't even fucking do! I'm finding those letters, Clayton, and when I do, so help me God, I may kill him."

The panic hits again, mostly because I think she means it. "Kill who, Mia? Baby, you're worrying me—"

"Samuel!" she replies sharply. "I can't talk about this anymore. Not tonight. I won't do anything stupid or reckless. I won't shoot anyone unless they're trying to break in. I promise."

"I can be there in ten minutes," I offer. It might kill me to walk out of this house again, to walk away from Annalee and what almost happened just a moment ago, but I will. Whatever is happening with Mia, she is clearly not herself right now. Or maybe it's like she said, and she finally *is* being herself. That might be scarier.

"No. I shouldn't have yelled at you. I'm just angry and hurt...and jealous. If you're with Annalee, it's where you ought to be. Stay there. I'll be fine. Just don't expect me in the office tomorrow. I'm going to be tearing this house apart from top to bottom."

"I can help you," I offer again. I mean it. I'd do anything for her or for Quentin.

"Yes, you can," she says with certainty. "Whatever it is

46

you're working on, whatever you're trying to do destroy him, keep going. Don't stop until you have it. When this is all done, I want him left with nothing...promise me that."

"Whatever it takes." It's not a promise I'm making lightly. Destroying Samuel has already cost me more than I was willing to give. I won't stop. No matter what it takes.

"Now, go seduce your wife. Or let her seduce you. We like that sometimes."

"That is really not what's happening here and for the love of God, just don't go there with me. I can't take it. Quentin is bad enough," I say to her. I don't hear her laugh, which worries me, but when she answers, I can hear the smile in her voice. It's enough.

"Good night, Clay. I love you."

"Love you too, Mia-mine," I reply. The nickname slips out, something our mother used to call her.

"You bastard. I thought I was done crying for the night."

My own eyes are burning a little. But I don't cry. I haven't. Not in a long time and I'm not going to start now. But Mia is a different matter altogether. "Maybe you need to cry. You can't bottle it up forever," I tell her.

"I can try," she protests lamely.

"It doesn't work. Take it from someone who knows... call me. Anytime. I will come right there if you need me."

"I know you will. Good night," she whispers softly and the phone clicks.

I place my phone on the counter and look at Annalee who clearly has questions. "I still don't know what's going on."

"Mia isn't suicidal?" she asks, a line of worry forming between her brows.

47

"No." I try to sound as certain and as reassuring as possible. "But she may need a lawyer if Samuel goes near her."

"Are you going over there?" Annalee asks softly. I can tell that she thinks I should, and maybe it's just wishful thinking on my part, but I can also tell that part of her doesn't want me to go.

"No." I'm not totally confident in the decision, but it's the best I've got. "I think I'll do more good for Mia by working this from a different angle...I didn't want to tip my hand, but I'm going to have to make Samuel give up control."

Annalee frowns at me. "Control of what?"

I've never talked to her about my plans for Samuel. I worry that I am saying too much, that when it all goes to hell, and it will, that she won't have the distance needed to be safe. But I need to say it to someone, and even after everything else, there's no one I trust more. "Everything—the house. Mama. The distillery...if we don't get him out of our lives—that's not an option. He will be out of our lives. One way or another."

She doesn't say anything for the longest time, just leaves me squirming under that measuring gaze. "Don't do anything stupid. Emma Grace needs you," she finally states.

It's a dangerous question to ask, but I have to know. "Just Emma Grace? Or do you still need me too, Annalee?"

"I needed you a year and a half ago," she says softly. "I needed you twelve months ago...even six months ago, if you'd looked at me then the way you looked at me tonight, my answer would be different."

"It's not too late," I reply, and I hate how desperate I sound.

48

"Isn't it? We can't do this, Clay. What just happened —this is confusing enough for Emma Grace without us acting like hormonal teenagers who can't figure out if we're broken up or not."

"What is confusing to her exactly? The fact that you threw me out?" There are some things that I shouldn't say to her. I understand why she did it. I understand why I didn't fight it. But the loneliness of it, the fucking misery of being separated from her, from my daughter—that kind of misery makes you mean. It makes you lash out and one hurt just builds on the other.

She squares her shoulders and levels an icy glare at me. "I asked you to move out, Clayton, but you left me a long time ago. You checked out. You didn't look at me, didn't talk to me, you sure as hell didn't touch me...living with you was like living with a damn ghost."

The accusation stings because I know it's true. It hadn't been by choice, it hadn't been because I didn't want to tell her everything. But struggling to keep the distillery afloat, to keep the mortgage paid and the roof over our heads, not to mention the possibility that things I'm doing could land me in prison—I'd wanted to spare her that.

"I never stopped loving you...not then and not now. What the hell else do you need from me?" I ask.

"The only thing I ever needed *was* you," she replies. "But all I got was this cold, distant stranger."

I take her hands. "I'm here now. I'm talking to you. I'm looking at you, and two minutes ago I had my hands on—"

"I know where your hands were!" she interrupts and pulls her hands free. "But what happens the next time life gets hard, Clayton? What happens the next time the business is in trouble or work is too stressful? You'll just shut me out again and we'll be back where we started!"

"Annalee, I don't want us to end this way."

Annalee crosses her arms over her chest and leans her head back, a sigh of deep exasperation escaping her. "You think I wanted this? I didn't, Clayton...I had a very different vision of where we'd be right now."

"I don't know how to fix this."

ANNALEE

"I don't think we can be fixed...not the way we were. Right now, we just have to focus on Emma Grace and move on." I feel like we've poked at our bruises enough for one night. We're not any better off than we were before. He's still keeping secrets and I'm still standing my ground, even if it is on knees that wobble. "You've got clothes upstairs still, if you want to change," I offer. I need him to go upstairs, I need him to be away from me for a moment so I can regain whatever semblance of balance I had before.

He loops the tie around his hand. It's an old habit, something I always teased him about. "You could come up with me," he offers.

I know that tone. I know that look. And God help me, my brain and my ovaries are at war over it. "That's not a good idea."

"And your date the other night?" he asks. There's a hardness in his tone, a cold and calculating look in his eyes. "Was that a good idea?"

I look away. I should be lying to him, should be

feeding his jealous. But that's Brit's way of doing things. Not mine. I can't. "No, it wasn't a good idea. It was an exercise in misery. Happy?"

"Nothing about that makes me happy," he replies. "I want to find him and rip his fucking throat out. You're not supposed to be with him."

"Am I supposed to be with you, then?" I ask with a bitter laugh. "Really, Clayton? Am I not entitled to try to have a life after you?"

He shoves his hands into his hair, that same familiar gesture that he makes every time he gets frustrated or doesn't know how to handle something. "I just need some time, Annalee. If you give me a little while, I can fix all this. Once it's done, I'll tell you everything. I promise."

"I can't," I respond. It hurts me to say it. It fucking breaks my heart all over again. "I keep holding on to this hope that I'll wake up and this will all be a bad dream, and everything will be like it was. But that's not going to happen. And I need to start living in the here and now and not some fantasy world where you love me the way I want you to...the truth of it is, Clayton, I only went out on a date with him because of you."

His gaze hardens. "You're going to have to explain that a little better. The logic of it is eluding me."

I roll my eyes. Of course, the logic of it eludes him. Hell, it eluded me. Goddamn Brit and her crazy plan. "Brit—."

"Well, that explains a lot!"

"Brit," I continue, "suggested that if I really wanted to know if you still cared, I should see whether or not it made you jealous to think of me seeing someone else."

"You can tell her it fucking worked."

"But it didn't." Did it piss him off? Yes. Sure it did. But there was no epiphany. There was no moment where he thought, I'll do whatever it takes to get her back. He was going on the same way he had before, just slightly grumpier. "You're still not willing to give an inch. You're still not willing to let me in."

"Annalee, everything I'm doing is to protect you...to keep you and Emma Grace safe. Mia, Quentin, Mama. There's so much at stake here. Do you honestly think I want to carry this alone?"

"I think you're going to, no matter what I say. So it's a pointless question." My reply might seem a little heartless, even mean. But I've got to stop hoping. I've got to accept the reality of our current situation and move on, no matter how much it hurts.

I can't look at him anymore, I realize. It just hurts too much. I turn to walk away, but his hand snakes out and grabs my arm, pulling me back, holding on to me like he can't quite bear to let go.

"Don't," he says. "Please, just don't."

"Clayton—" I begin, but I realize I don't have anything to say. He's holding me to him, our wet clothes plastered together. I can feel the heat of him, the hardness of him against me. It feels so good and so tempting.

When he kisses me, I can't think. I can't breathe. I can't do anything but feel his lips on me, the slide of his tongue between my lips, penetrating, blatantly sexual. His hands drift down to my ass, cupping each cheek and pressing into me. I can feel the thick length of him, hard and full against me. He rocks his hips and all I can think of is how good it would feel for him to be inside me.

I can't do this. I'm weakening, falling under his spell. It takes everything in me to push him back. I press my hands against his chest and he steps back, reluctantly.

"I can't help wanting you," I tell him. "But wanting

you doesn't make you good for me. *You're not good for me right now.* You have to go...now."

"Annalee." He just says my name. Nothing else. He looks at me for the longest time and then just turns on his heels and leaves.

I watch him walk out and it takes everything I have in me not to call him back, not to strip my clothes off and attack him naked in the foyer. I follow after him, just to the kitchen door and before I can catch myself, I say something that I know I'll regret. "The final papers should be here by the end of next week. You wanted time, Clayton, and that's what I'm willing to give you. Once I sign them, there's no going back."

He stops in his tracks. He doesn't look back at me. Just stands there for a moment and lets that sink in. After a moment, he gives a brief nod and heads for the door.

I've fucked up. I've given him another chance to break my heart, because if he doesn't tell me the truth in the next ten days, then I'll have to say goodbye to those hopes and dreams all over again.

I head back into the kitchen and open the freezer door. There's a pint of Ben and Jerry's in there that belongs to Emma Grace. I'm going to have to owe her one. I'm going to eat the whole damn thing.

Four

CLAYTON

Pulling into the parking lot of my shithole condo, I sit there in the car so fucking mad I can't see straight. Of course it doesn't help that my damn dick is still so hard I'll do myself permanent injury if I try to walk from the car to the front door.

It isn't just being horny. It isn't just that I haven't been touched by anything softer than my own damn hand in more than a year. It's her—it's always been her. She twists me up in knots and turns me inside out.

I lean the seat back and just stare up through the moon roof of the car for a minute. It was something we used to do, long before Emma Grace came along. A country road on a clear night in my old car, and we'd stay like that for hours. Until she climbed over the console and straddled me.

I grip the steering wheel in a mixture of frustration and anger. My mind keeps supplying all those tempting images of her, of us together. And it's not doing a goddamn thing to relieve my current physical misery.

Liquor. If I can't have what I want, I decide, I'll just drink until I don't fucking care. Getting out of the car, I walk to the front door, but as I insert the key into the lock, the door swings inward.

Fuck.

There, sitting in my living room like he's got every fucking right to be there, is Samuel Darcy.

"I'm in no goddamn mood to deal with you tonight. You need to leave and you need to do it now," I tell him.

"I'm concerned about your sister," he says, acting as if I hadn't just told him to get the fuck out.

"Mia's a big girl. She can take care of herself," I reply. I need that drink now more than ever. I walk into the kitchen and open the cupboard. I pull down a half-full bottle of Maker's Mark. I don't even bother with a glass, just carry the bottle back to the living room with me.

"You ought to be ashamed of yourself for drinking that," Samuel scolds. "Fire Creek is better."

"Since we're in a shortage, I figured I'd buy something readily available and save our bottles for paying customers...more to the point, I didn't ask your fucking opinion. Get out."

"Son, I will go when I am goddamn ready," he replies.

"Then say what you mean to and go." I take a healthy swig of the bourbon, letting it burn all the way down. Maybe it'll put out the other fires raging inside me.

"She's getting tangled up with Bennett Hayes again. I don't need to tell you what a disaster that could be," Samuel states. "It'd be a shame for Mia to lose her head over this man and for poor Patricia to have no one to properly look after her."

"She's a grown woman—her choice and her business.

And for the record, no one will ever take better care of Mama than Mia does. Like you'd fucking know, of course. What rent-a-slut did you tear yourself away from tonight to come here?" My reply is terse. I want him gone. I'm freaked the hell out by the fact that he's been in my house, alone here to go through whatever the fuck he feels like, while I'm away. I make a mental note to change the locks.

"Clayton," he says smoothly. "I know that we don't see eye to eye on a lot of things—"

"On anything, old man."

He goes on as if I didn't just interrupt and insult him.

"The fact of the matter is, I have Mia's and the distillery's best interest at heart. There's a lot of old gossip...wives' tales, if you will, about whether or not the Hayes family is entitled to a piece of the Fire Creek legacy. The two of them being together will only fuel that fire."

"That fire rages out of control for every resident of Fontaine, mostly because they all know it's true. I don't know the particulars, but hell, even *I* know it's true. If someone says a Darcy, or at least a Darcy from previous generations, did something shady...hell, that's just like saying the sky is blue in my book. You'll have to do better than that."

Samuel's expression hardens, and for just a second, I can see the monster in him. "He doesn't want her. He just wants what she can give him access to. I hate to see her waste herself on a man like that...I've been trying to get her to go with me to the Annual Bourbon Association gala. There are some people in the industry that it would be very beneficial—"

I stand up and open the door. "She's not your whore. You're not her pimp. You don't get to turn her out. Go."

"Clayton—"

"You get the fuck out. If I have to throw you out, I'm

going to do it with a lot more force than either of us will like."

Samuel gets to his feet, straightens his suit jacket and tie and looks at me as if he's disappointed in me. Like he has the right. "I had thought with your love of Fire Creek, you'd be more receptive to doing what it takes to make the distillery a success."

"I do love Fire Creek. But I love my family more. I'm actually capable of love. That's the difference between us." He moves past me toward the door, but just as his feet pause at the threshold, I say one more thing to him. "If you ever darken my door again, I'll put a bullet in you. Are we clear?"

He doesn't acknowledge the statement just walks on toward the shiny new Mercedes that he's leased for himself. I know he leased it because he can't afford to buy it, the shit. I watch him drive off and take another long pull from the bottle. That son of a bitch will burn if it's the last thing I do.

Five

CLAYTON

I'm back in the office the next day. It's after lunch, which I avoided like the damn plague. Half a fifth of bourbon makes the idea of food surprisingly unpalatable. I'm so hungover I could die. Not to mention the fact that Annalee left me with my balls tied in a knot and then Samuel showed up like shit sprinkles on a dirt cake.

The door to my office opens and Quentin walks in. The smell of the sour mash cooking up wafts in with him, and I have to question whether I finished off the bourbon or whether it finished off me.

"You look like ass," Quentin states.

"I feel like it too. What do you want?"

"I went by the house this morning. I have no idea what's going on but it looks like a damned tornado went through it. Mia has shit torn out all over the place...she looks a little crazed."

Recalling the conversation with her the night before, I

sigh. Everything is coming to head—with Mia and Bennett, with our shithead father, and now Annalee has given me a deadline. "If you've got anything on Samuel I can use, I need it now. I'd like to wait, to gather a little more evidence before I go in for the final push, but time is a luxury we don't have anymore."

"It isn't much. The lead in Knoxville didn't pan out... or maybe they just chickened out. So we're left with a stripper in Vegas, but no one cares about that. There's the gambling and kickbacks from our state representative, but dragging a politician into this mess could bite us in the ass," Quentin points out. "We need the big stuff that you won't even tell me about, and I don't know how to get it."

It was true. Pissing off politicians when you were in the liquor business was never a good idea. As for the big stuff, I still have no proof, only speculation. He was the last person to see Katherine Shelby alive, but a missing debutante and a paint job on his boat isn't enough to get him charged. "I've got the tax records," I reply. "I've got the documented affairs from before Mama's accident, the final tally of what's left of her money after he spent it all on his mistresses."

Quentin makes a disgusted sound. "Do I want to know how much?"

I pull the statement from a file in my desk drawer and lay it in front of Quentin. "Less than twenty thousand. He ran through a ten-million-dollar estate like it was beer money at the track. There's still a couple million in another trust which matures in about five months. That would pay for her caregivers for the rest of her life...or it would give Samuel one hell of a weekend."

Looking over the piece of paper, Quentin's jaw clenches with fury. "Cars, clothes, apartments, jewelry, trips to Europe and the Bahamas! He's been taking his whores on pleasure cruises while we've been working our asses off? And Mia...for the love of God! She hasn't left Fontaine other than a day trip to Lexington, or back when she was commuting to school, in over a decade!"

I know that. I know every bit of it straight to my soul, but it won't give us the leverage we need. "It's not enough...we might be able to get him to give up the distillery, but with the promise of Mama's trust, he won't forfeit guardianship of her...and that's nonnegotiable right now," I reply coolly.

Quentin crosses his arms over his chest and tips the chair back. It's his thinking pose, even as a kid, he'd sit like that whenever he was working something out in his head.

"What's going on in your head, Quentin?"

"The investor I mentioned," he offers. "He's in."

"He's got the ready capital to just buy in? Who is this?"

"A friend," Quentin hedges. "Pro football, wants to retire while his knees will still support him."

Clayton shook his head. "I don't know. We need long term here. Not someone who's going to get bored and leave us floundering."

"He's local, or at least he used to be. He's coming back to Kentucky for good and wants to be involved in local enterprises."

I've got a good idea of just who Quentin is talking about and it's concerning, at the very least. Quentin has a bent toward being wild and reckless himself. The last thing he needs is someone else with those same qualities involved in the day-to-day operations of the distillery. "Mallory?"

Quentin nods. "Keep it quiet. He hasn't announced his retirement officially yet."

A soft knock at the office door keeps me from saying anything more. Annalee is standing in the doorway.

Quentin gets up and immediately moves toward the door. "I've got that thing that I was supposed to do...for the other thing."

"Coward," I accuse softly.

"Fuck, yes," Quentin answers and vanishes swiftly.

I'm not watching my brother's retreat. My eyes on her, locked and unmoving. *My wife*, or at least she would be for a little while longer.

"You look awful," she says softly as she comes in and takes a seat.

I shrug. I'm hungover. It goes with the territory. "I feel it. I can still drink like I'm twenty...unfortunately, I recover like I'm eighty."

"You got drunk?"

I fight the impulse to roll my eyes at her scandalized tone. It would hurt too bad. "There's two cures for blue balls, Annalee. For the record, bourbon was my second choice."

I watch her, noting the blush that steals over her cheeks. It's not embarrassment putting it there. She's still just as hot for me as I am for her, even if she is dressed like a schoolteacher. In jeans and a simple sweater, she's a far cry from the pseudo-hippy I met in while in grad school. That girl would have shared the bourbon with me and then taught me lessons on the Kama Sutra.

Remembering the long, gypsy hair and the crazy clothes she wore, half of which had come from thrift stores, I smile in spite of myself. *More than half probably*. But it didn't matter. I saw her the night that Kentucky beat Utah to go on to the championship game. She'd been dancing around a burning couch on the lawn of my apartment building.

There was something about her, about the way she moved, the abandon of it all that had called to me. The party had been my roommate's idea. I was supposed to be studying. It's the only time in my life that doing the wrong thing ever truly went in my favor. One look at her and that was it. I convinced her to go out with me, and I never looked back.

On our first date, she'd confessed to me that she didn't even know what people were celebrating, but it was free beer and looked like a good time. She'd just joined in. Wild, unfettered, and more drunk on life than on the cheap beer flowing from a dozen kegs up and down the street, I'd never met anyone like her before.

"When did we get old, Ann?" I ask. "We used to drink like fish, fuck like rabbits and fight like the damn devil... where did all that go?"

She laughs, just as I'd intended. "We stopped most of that after Emma Grace came along. She demanded a lot of attention from both of us. She has a dance recital this weekend."

It's already marked on my calendar. "She told me. I'll be there."

Annalee looks down at her feet, clearly uncomfortable. "I wanted to apologize for last night...for all of it. What happened—it shouldn't have. And for the other day, what I said to you about the date, about going out with someone...I shouldn't have told you that. But it feels weird to keep things from you," she admits. "I said it to make you jealous, and it was a stupid, childish, and selfish thing to do."

I curse under my breath and pinch the bridge of my nose. My head pounding like a damn steam train. "I have to apologize too." It was a hard thing for me to say. "It's not my place to question you anymore about where you're going or what you're doing...or who you're doing it with."

"Old habits," she offers.

"Something like that," I agree. Even miserable and hungover, even under the crushing weight of the knowledge that I might lose her forever, I want her. I want to lose myself in her, to inhale the scent of her and taste her on my tongue.

It must have shown on my face, some hint of what I was feeling, because as she meets my gaze, the silence between us shifts and changes. It's charged now with something that neither one of us will dare to name. If we do, I'll have her naked on this desk and be balls deep inside her before either of us can have a chance to think twice. "As for everything else that happened...the only thing I'm sorry for is that we didn't finish what we started."

She looks away abruptly. "Clayton—"

"I don't regret it," I insist, and my tone is more forceful than I intended for it to be. "I ought to, but I don't. If my asshole brother wasn't just down the hall and two dozen workers just a floor below, I'd show you just how much I don't regret it."

She blinks at me, clearly unprepared for the confession. Whatever else is going on between us, she still wants me. I seize onto that. It's the only hope I have.

Her voice is breathless as she abruptly changes the subject, "I thought I'd go check on Mia. I know you're worried about her."

It was a peace offering and I take it for that. I sigh and nod. "Thank you. Quentin went up there earlier but she won't talk to him the way she'd talk to you."

Annalee laughs. "You mean Mr. Sensitivity? Why the hell not?"

There is nothing constructive to add to that. Quentin

has always been pretty oblivious when it comes to women he doesn't intend to sleep with. I want to tell her how much it means to me that she's looking out for Mia, that she's still a part of the family regardless of what's happening between us. Maybe if I wasn't nursing the mother of all hangovers it would be different, or maybe if she didn't have me tied in so many goddamn knots I can't see straight. "I don't know how to fix this for her," I admit gruffly.

"She won't let you fix it," Annalee replies. "And Mia's my family too. Not by blood, not even by marriage for very much longer, but she'll always be my family."

"Not another damn word about that. There's no expiration date on this now. You gave me an option last night...a deadline. I will make it, Annalee. Whatever I have to do, by the time those papers are in your hand, this is all going to look very different."

She doesn't take umbrage at that, but she doesn't acknowledge my resolve either. "I'm not sure who I'm reminding anyway...me or you. Emma Grace has dance practice after her field trip, so if I'm going to spend any time at all with Mia, I should go now."

I watch her get up and walk toward the door. No one moves like her, I think to myself again. Whether it's the yoga she's addicted to, the dance classes she'd taken when she was younger, or just her own innate grace, it has always been a sight I appreciated.

"Wait."

She turns back, glancing over her shoulder at me. "What?"

I don't have a reason, other than that I just wasn't ready to see her leave. "I just wanted to look at you."

"There's not much to see," she protests.

I get up from the desk and move toward her until

we're standing less than a breath apart. "You're wrong about that...there's you."

She exhales, the sound fractured and wounded. "Damn you, Clayton."

I touch her face, stroking the softness of her cheek and then sliding my thumb over her lower lip. "Do you remember the night we met? Sitting in that shithole of a diner talking for hours?"

She meets my gaze steadily, but there's a slight tremor in her. I can feel it when I touch her. "I remember everything," she utters.

"And then driving home, parking in front of your house." I pause for a second. "And a good night kiss that turned into so much more."

"Clayton, we can't go back...we're not those people anymore," she whispers.

"We are," I insist. I press her back against the door, letting her feel how much I want her, how hard I am for her. "I want you the same way now that I did then. I crave you like I always did. Tell me you don't feel that way!"

"Don't do this to me, Clayton," she whispers brokenly.

"What am I doing, Annalee?"

"Don't be the man now that I needed a year ago. Don't offer me what I wanted and needed when it's probably too damned late!"

She pushes me away, and I let her. Mostly because I can see the hurt in her. Beyond the confusion, beyond the need that won't leave either one of us alone, I know she's still hurting and the last thing I want to do is hurt her more. She turns and flees, her heels clicking on the floor as she all but runs from me.

I go back to my desk and lean back in the chair, scrubbing my hands over my face. There is too much between us. Too much for me to let go and too much for her to look past.

The fury inside me, the controlled rage that I normally keep locked down tight, roars to life. With a sweep of my arm, I've cleared the top of the desk. The phone crashes to the floor, papers flutter in the air before coming to rest on the ground. It doesn't make me feel any better. Neither do the litany of curses that follow. It's the second time in a week my destructive temper has escaped me. It's a record.

Six

ANNALEE

I arrive at the family home and Evelyn, the lady who normally stays with Patricia, answers the door. She looks at me with a worried frown. "I don't know what has my baby so tore up, but whatever it is, it ain't good!"

"Where is she, Evelyn?" I ask. I'm still raw from the face-off with Clayton in his office. Even when we're not trying to hurt one another, we do. Maybe focusing on Mia's issues instead of my own will help.

"She's upstairs in her mama's old room. She has torn this house apart! Everything in it is upside down...not that it doesn't need to be. They've been living in this house like it's a museum for far too long."

I move past Evelyn toward the stairs. She's probably right about all of that. In a lot of ways, even though they've all gone on and done other things, for Mia, Quentin, and Clayton, it's like a part of them froze in time with Patricia.

I enter the bedroom and note the dated decor. Even before the accident, Patricia had been talking about wanting to update and get rid of the Laura Ashley wallpaper and bedding. The heavy oak furniture with its early American motif is just as out of fashion. But it's not the decor that has me stopping in my tracks. Mia is sitting on the floor, cross-legged, surrounded by boxes. Her hair is wild, her face is streaked with dust and she appears to be wearing clothes more appropriate to clubbing than housework. She's so focused on the task in front of her that she hasn't even realized I'm in the room.

"Can I help?" I ask softly.

Mia looks up at me and instantly, her eyebrow goes up speculatively. "You look rested," she says, and there's a world of innuendo in her tone.

"He did not spend the night. I did not sleep with him," I reply, keeping my answers concise and completely honest. "Stop poking at my love life and I won't poke at yours."

Mia cocks her head to the side and considers it for a moment. "Done."

"So what am I looking for?" I ask her.

"Letters. Handwritten to my mother or father from Barbara Shelby. They may or may not be signed."

I take a seat on one of the upholstered chairs that flank the dresser and grab one of the plastic storage totes. "Got it. Am I going to be grossed out by them?"

"Probably."

I wipe the dust off the top of the tote before opening it. I start sifting through the contents, piece by piece. It's depressing and sad to think that the person who put these things in a box is lying downstairs, probably completely unaware of anything going around on her. Of course, my more immediate concerns are for Mia. Whatever is going on with her, it's bad. I've never seen her like this. "Not to be too much of a nanny here but, have you slept? Or showered?"

"No, and I'm hot. Sweating like a whore in church. There's a lot of things you shouldn't be poking at right now," Mia replies pointedly.

There's a lot of warning packed into that tone. "Fair enough."

We work in silence for the longest time, each one of us sorting through years of memories. The tedium isn't what's getting to me. Picking out school papers, awards that each of her children had received that had been carefully filed away, bills paid. All the little pieces of a life that just stopped. It never ended. Just stopped.

My thoughts must have mirrored Mia's because she looks up at me. There are no tears in her eyes, not because she doesn't need to shed them, but more than likely because she's already cried out her quota.

"This is what's left of her. This, right here, all these plans and tasks...I don't want this to be someday. I don't want to look up and realize that I let my whole life be an accumulation of things that I thought I would do or have someday."

I meet Mia's gaze and the papers I've been shuffling still in my hand. I'd hurt for Clayton when Patricia was in that accident, I'd cried for him when he wouldn't in the aftermath. We hadn't even been together that long, but I'd known then how much it was cutting him, how much it hurt with every progressively negative report from every doctor that examined her. Persistent vegetative state was the final word, but no one could explain why. And Mia has been left here, alone for the most part, caring for a woman with no end in sight.

"Mia, I don't know what happened here last night," I

begin, but it's hard to speak past the lump that has formed in my throat. Apparently all the Darcys want to make me an emotional wreck today. "Or what happened here the night you intended to run away with him...but I do know, that in spite of everything, these last two weeks I have seen you smile more, laugh more, and live more than I have in the twelve years that I have known you."

A pained expression crosses Mia's face, a kind of agony that I am all too familiar with. If Clayton is the love of my life, then surely Bennett Hayes is hers. I've always known that Mia was hurting, that she was lonely and unhappy being so isolated, but I'd never known just how much. I hadn't allowed myself to see it, if I'm honest. Neither had Clayton or Quentin. We've all just gone about our business and left Mia to fend for herself. Being hit with the realization that you've been an entitled, self-indulgent shit to someone you actually care for is a bitter pill to swallow.

Mia is miserable and if Bennett Hayes can undo that, if he can break through that hard, icy shell Mia has been wearing for years, I'll be the first one in line to cheer him on. Reaching into the box on my lap, I pull out a photo and hold it up to Mia. "For the last week and half, you've been this girl. A little older and a little wiser...well, *maybe* a little wiser. But I've never known the girl in this picture. I've never seen your eyes sparkle like this...not until recently."

There is a long pause, silence stretches in the room. Finally, Mia asks, "Do you regret it?"

"Regret what?" I respond. It's a stalling tactic. I know exactly what she is talking about. The conversation has turned and this is no longer solely about Mia and Bennett. Now it's Clayton and myself under the microscope.

Mia's expression tells me in no uncertain terms that

she isn't buying the dumb act. "Do you regret leaving my brother?"

She won't let me off without giving her a straight answer. Since I've birthed one of their ilk, I know all about how hardheaded and strong willed a Darcy female can be. Still, I try to keep my answer vague, more to protect my bruised feelings than because I feel like she's prying. "I regret feeling like I had no other option."

"That's not really an answer. Do you miss Clayton? Do you think about him and about how things might have been, or could still be, different?"

She's given me a question I can't dodge. *Fuck.* "I thought we weren't going to poke at this," I hedge, throwing Mia's own words back in her face.

"Changed my mind," Mia says with a shrug, as if she is perfectly entitled to so do.

A dozen and one things cross my mind. The months of silence and distance, the invisible wall that Clayton constructed between us for reasons he couldn't or wouldn't explain. But it's the encounter in the kitchen the previous night, the weight of his hands and the heat of his mouth on hers, the way we talked like we used to, all of that is there at the forefront of my mind. Yes. I regret it. Every day in a dozen different ways since he moved out of the house, I regret it.

"Of course, I do. I love him. I will always love him... but somehow, it just stopped being what it was supposed to be for us. He got quiet and distant, and I felt like a shadow moving through his life. Whatever was in his head, whatever was consuming him...he wouldn't share that with me."

Mia shakes her head at me, like I'm being an idiot. Maybe I am.

"Clay doesn't do a whole lot of sharing, Annalee," she says pointedly. "That's not who he is. He's the fixer. Hell, that's why you're here right now!"

I can't talk about it anymore, I can't look at it anymore. It's like broken tempered glass. It's all still together, each of those million broken pieces clinging together against all odds, but one more staggering blow, and the pieces will scatter and I'll never put them all together again.

"I know that, Mia. I've always known that about him...but how he related to the rest of the world was not how he was supposed to relate to me. I was his wife. I deserved to have a piece of him that was just mine."

"I'm sorry," Mia said. "I wish I could make it better."

I force my tone to soften, realizing that I've spoken to her far too harshly when she is clearly in a fragile state herself. I take a deep breath and force the clenched muscles in my body to ease before they just snap. Mia isn't trying to hurt me, but then neither is Clayton. It still feels like they've both left a mark though. "We all wish that for the people we love. Whatever happens for Clayton and me, you're my family. Got it?"

Mia nods. "I got it. And I'm guessing that it's time to pick up Emma Grace from...what is it today? Dance, Girl Scouts?"

Thankful for the reprieve, I answer with a smile. "A field trip to the candy factory in Bardstown. What the hell happened to just going to school?"

I get up from the chair and place the box back on the floor. There is no point in uttering a goodbye, Mia is already engrossed in the next box. She is on a mission like a woman possessed.

I leave, slipping out before Evelyn can corner me and demand my accounting of how I think her baby girl is doing. I'm hoping against hope that Mia finds what she needs, that all of that digging through the baggage of their lives and their tragedies isn't for nothing. I climb into my minivan to go and pick up Emma Grace and glance in the mirror. "I hope we all do."

CLAYTON

It was dark by the time I parked in front of my condo again. The day had gone by at a crawl and I still felt like ass. Going through the front door, it was a relief not to see Samuel there or to have any other unexpected guests. All I want is to take enough Tylenol to fell a horse and guzzle water by the gallon.

Stepping into the kitchen, I grab one of the two kitchen towels that I actually own and fill it with ice which I immediately press to my aching head. "Fucking hell! I am never drinking again." It's a lie. I knew it was the minute I uttered the words, but at the moment they're gospel.

Moving to the couch, I settle in, lean my head back and close my eyes against the glare. I'm too damn old to feel this way and to be this damn stupid. From across the room, where I dropped my jacket and briefcase as soon as I walked in, I heard my phone ring. For about two seconds, I consider not answering.

I can't do it. It could be Annalee, though I doubt it. It could be any one of the half dozen people who have been feeding me info about Samuel. Or it could be Mia. Right now, that's my biggest concern. Annalee had sent me a text in the afternoon stating that whatever had happened with Mia she was still "fragile." I don't know exactly what that means, but I sure as hell don't like it.

In the end, I ignore my aching head and my less-than-happy stomach and cross the room to answer the phone. I don't recognize the number which doesn't bode well.

"Clayton?"

I know that voice. If Bennett Hayes is calling me there's a damn good reason. "Yes."

"It's Bennett Hayes. Mia is at my house and will be for at least the next twenty-four hours. Your father is with Patricia, so you probably want to get somebody on that."

Son of a bitch. This isn't good. There is nothing about this that can possibly be good. "Is Mia hurt?"

I can hear the hesitation in Bennett's voice before he answers. "Physically? No. I don't think so. But that son of a bitch is going to hell for the emotional shit he's put her through."

Truer words were never spoken. The fact that I'm not totally clear on what exactly he's talking about worries me more than a little. "That's an understatement...I know what he is, Hayes. I've known for a long time. I'm working on that, but taking down someone who is a professional liar like Samuel isn't easy."

Bennett gets quiet on the other end for a second. I can all but hear the wheels turning. When he speaks again, he asks a question I wasn't expecting. "What do you need?"

It's an easy enough answer to give. It's a harder thing to lay hands on. "Something damaging enough to kill his social status. If he thinks he's losing that, he'll come to heel quick enough."

Bennett sighs and then says in a resigned voice, "I need you to meet me at my brother's farm in an hour."

"Will I be leaving it alive?" Emmitt Hayes is a crazy bastard. Big, mean and possibly ugly. It's hard to tell under his lumberjack beard. The one thing I do know is that he hates everything Darcy. If he sees me roll up to his front door, I'm liable to get shot, if not worse.

"Alive, yes. Unscathed? Don't get out of your car unless I'm there."

I can hear the smile in Bennett's voice when he answers. The bastard is enjoying himself. "Fine," I agree.

There are no goodbyes. The call just ends abruptly. I go into the kitchen, dump the makeshift ice pack in the sink and grab some Tylenol from the cabinet and a bottle of water from the fridge. They probably won't help, but at this point, they can't hurt. It's a good thirty minutes to the Hayes farm.

I pick up my phone again and call Annalee. She picks up after one ring. I can hear Emma Grace giggling in the background.

"I need a favor," I say immediately.

"What is it?"

"I hate to ask, but I need you to go over to Mama's for a while. Apparently, Mia either left under her own steam or Samuel kicked her out. Anyway, he's there with Mama right now, so I'm on my way over to evict his ass. But after that, I've got to go meet Emmitt Hayes and probably get my ass handed to me."

I realize I've said way too much and just clam up. Annalee is quiet for a minute. "Clayton, I don't like the idea of you going out there. I like Bennett just fine. And I think Savannah is great. I wouldn't trust Carter with anything female, but I don't think he's a bad guy. Emmitt...well, he's not bad, but his hatred of you runs deep."

"I'm aware. Bennett will be there too. It should be safe...I think. I hope."

"I've got to get myself and Emma Grace dressed. I'll be there as soon as I can."

She has to get dressed. That's the only part of that last statement that seems to be resonating with me. Like the poor, pathetic, horny bastard I am, I ask, "So, what are you wearing?"

"Clayton Joseph Darcy, we are not having that conversation!" she hisses.

"Just tell me, do you have on panties?"

She sighs into the phone. "Yes."

"Don't lie to me, Annalee. I can tell. You're wearing a pair of yoga pants, I'd lay odds on it, and given how well I know your habits, you don't have on any underwear beneath them, do you?"

There's no response. Just silence coming from the phone. It's confirmation enough.

After a long pause, she says, "This is a pointless conversation."

"Oh, there's a point to it. I have no idea what I'm going to the Hayes farm for, but if it's what I think it is... you and I will be having a long talk. After that talk, we'll be together, but we won't be talking at all. You just count on it."

"I'll be at your mama's house in about twenty minutes."

The call ends abruptly. I pushed her. I know I did. And if this plays out the way I need it to, I'll be doing a hell of a lot more than that.

I scroll through my contacts and call Evelyn's phone. She answers after the first ring.

"Evelyn, are you at the house?"

"I'm pulling into the driveway right now," she replies.

"Go in, pack an overnight bag for Mia and then just

leave. Don't talk to Samuel, don't even look at him. I'm on my way there."

"Your mama needs to be turned and fed," she protests.

"I'll turn her when I get there and Annalee can take care of the tube feeding."

Evelyn gets quiet for a second. "Where's my baby girl, Clayton? And don't you lie to me!"

I smile in spite of myself. Evelyn was our housekeeper long before she became Mama's caregiver. She ran roughshod over me and Quentin as kids, but she coddled and spoiled Mia like there was no tomorrow. "She's fine, Evelyn. She's at Bennett's house, but I don't know how long she'll be staying there. It's okay. I'm going to fix this."

"All right."

I grab my keys and head out to the car. It's a short drive to my mother's house. I'll never call it Samuel's. He hasn't actually lived there since her accident anyway. When I pull into the drive, I see at least three vehicles. Mia's rental car is there. I don't know how she got to Bennett's house, but she didn't drive. Evelyn is parked beside her. The third car is Samuel's new Mercedes. I walk past it and up the back steps to the kitchen door, resisting the urge to key the paint. It's a childish impulse and point-less anyway since it's my hard work at Fire Creek that's paying for the damned thing.

I enter the house through the kitchen door. Evelyn is standing there at the counter looking worried.

"He's looking awfully pleased with himself," she says. "He only ever looks like that when he's hurt somebody."

"I don't know the details yet either. If I did, I'd tell you. Put Mia's bag in my car and go on home for the night. Between myself and Annalee, we've got Mama covered for the evening."

"Teresa will be back tomorrow night," Evelyn offers.

When she continues, her tone is a little more strident. "And I'm coming back here tomorrow no matter what you say. I don't take care of Patricia because you pay me to. I take care of Patricia because I love her and because I love you all."

I give the woman a hug. "I know all that. And we appreciate every bit of it, and we love you too. So, before you hear me and Samuel screaming at one another, and me saying words you'll want to wash my mouth out for, just go on home for tonight."

She pats me on the cheek. "You are a good boy, Clayton. You might have to do some bad things to get rid of that son of a bitch, but you're doing it for all the right reasons."

It's like she just reached inside me and pulled out my heart. That's what happens when you talk to people who've known you since birth. "Thank you, Evelyn."

I watch her head out the back door toward my car, Mia's bag in tow. I take a deep breath and prepare myself for the confrontation to come. I'm not a hundred percent. Hell, I'm not even at seventy-five. Hungover and wrung out, I've got to face the fucker. Jesus Christ, could this have come at a worse time?

I knew Samuel wouldn't be in the former study which has been converted into a room for Mama. He'd die before walking in there. Whenever he comes to the house he sticks to the kitchen or the formal living room, places where he doesn't have to acknowledge the pitiful shell of the woman he married and ruined.

Sure enough, that's where I find him. "Get out."

He raises an eyebrow at me. "This is my house, son. You don't get to throw me out of it."

"That's funny, because you haven't paid taxes on it over two years," I tell him. "I have proof of that, in case you're wondering. I've got proof of a lot of things that can make your life a lot less cushy and your social calendar a lot less full. I'll use everything I've got, too."

Samuel laughs at that. "I know you're not threatening me, boy. You don't have the balls for it."

Quentin hid the guns when he came over to check on Mia. It's a damn good thing I don't know where. "You'd be surprised what I have the balls to do. Annalee is coming over to stay with Mama, and you are getting the hell out. If you don't, I'll tell Erica all about the little jaunt to Los Cabos that you have planned...I'll also tell her about the younger, fresher model you have lined up to take her place."

Samuel's gaze hardens. He's never been one to take well to someone else having the power. "I know you're not spying on me," he says. "You're not that goddamn stupid."

I laugh. "As crooked as you are, I'd be stupid not to. Get out. If I have to tell you again, I'll throw you out."

"You'll regret crossing me, Clayton. I promise you that much. I can make your life hell, and if you think being my son affords you any sort of protection or leeway, you're wrong," he warns.

"The only thing being your son ever afforded me was the mistrust of others...well-founded since I've discovered I can be just as crooked as you," I reply. "I won't hesitate to throw you bodily from this house. If you happen to snap your neck in the process—well, accidents, happen, don't they?"

He gets up and moves toward the door, "For the record, I'm leaving because I want to...not because of your threats."

"I don't care why you go, as long as you do."

When Samuel is gone, I walk into the other room to

check on Mama. I don't know how long she's been lying on her side, but I'm pretty sure it's been too long. Using the underpad beneath her, I shift her onto her other side and prop a pillow beneath her. Her hand falls onto mine.

For just a moment, I hold on to it.

"I'm trying, Mama. I promise you, if it's the last thing I do, I will get that son of a bitch out of all of our lives."

There's the faintest tremor in her hand. I freeze, my eyes glued to her face. There's nothing, no indication that she's hearing or responding, but her hand moves again in mine, just the slightest flexing of her finger.

I can't breathe. "Mama, please, just one more time. Let me know you're doing that on purpose."

I wait for what seems like an hour, but it's only minutes. I wait until I hear the excited chatter of Emma Grace running inside and Annalee moving behind her, urging her to be quiet. Mama hasn't moved again and I begin to question whether or not she really did it all. Maybe it was just wishful thinking.

Annalee is standing in the doorway looking at me. I meet her gaze and it must have shown on my face. "Are you okay?" she asks.

I nod. If it happened, if it was real, it isn't something I can tell anyone. Not yet. I need more info. More proof. I need something that doesn't just make me look desperate and crazy.

"I'm fine," I lie.

Emma Grace comes in, rushing past me. She climbs up into the chair beside Mama's bed and opens one of her many books to read her a bedtime story. The munchkin has been doing that since before she could read. She used to just make it up. That's something else I have to be grateful to Annalee for. If it weren't for her, I don't know that it would have ever dawned on me to try and build a relationship between our child and a woman who could never respond to her, even if that woman was her grandmother.

I remember going to my own grandparents' house. I hadn't really understood then about money, about those who have it and those who don't. But they'd had it in spades. Still, it had been a warmer and much more inviting place than home, at least when Samuel was present. If Mama had responded, if there was something happening there, and Emma Grace could have that feeling of the complete and unconditional love of a grandparent, there's nothing I wouldn't do to give it to her.

Turning back to Annalee, I say, "I need to get going. If this is as big as I think it could be, I can't afford to piss them off by being late."

I move toward the door, but as I start to brush past her, her hand catches mine. She holds on to me for just a moment. It isn't much, but God above, it feels good. It feels like, for just a moment, we're a team again. Not fighting one another, not trying to hold on or let go. For that moment, we just are.

"Be careful," she whispers.

"I will," I promise. And as much as it hurts to do it, I pull away from her long enough to give Emma Grace a big hug and a loud kiss. "Be good while I'm gone. I'll see you in a bit."

ANNALEE

After Clayton leaves, I move over to Patricia's bedside and look down at her. I've spent a lot of time with her over the past few weeks, but because I'm not with her every day, I see things that others don't. The subtle tension in her features that tells me she's *there*. No, she's not in full control yet, but something is happening. Trapped in that shell, she's waking up. And I have the distinct feeling that she just did something to let Clayton know that.

"Emma Grace, you can read to your grandma later. Can you go to the living room and watch TV?"

Emma Grace looks at me as if I've asked her to move a mountain. I raise my eyebrow at her, and she lets out a huffing breath accompanied by an eye roll. "Fine."

When she's gone, I look back at Patricia, and even though I know she won't answer me, I have to ask. "What did you do, Patricia?"

Of course, there is no answer. I wasn't expecting one, but I think it's important to talk to her like she could answer.

"I know you're in there and I know you're hearing every word I say to you, so I'm going to be blunt. They need you. All of your children...right *now*, they need you. So whatever it takes, however hard you have to fight," I urge. "Come back to them."

There's a slight fluttering of her eyelids, but they don't open. Doctors would say it's simply nerves, that it's not a response, not an indication of awareness. *Fuck 'em*, I think. What do they know?

From one mother to another, I know that she knows they're hurting. Nothing will convince me otherwise.

I settle back into the chair while Emma Grace watches television in the living room. I'll get it out of him. Whatever she did, I'll get it out of him and I'll add it to the catalog of other things I've seen.

For the longest time, I've thought Patricia was misdiagnosed. They said she was in a vegetative state, but I've been reading about Locked-In Syndrome and I can't help but feel that's what's happening here. Samuel hasn't been exactly champing at the bit to have her re-evaluated. In fact, that asshole has been pretty content to just let her rot here while he goes out and lives the high life.

Clayton will fix it. Somehow, I know he will. I just pray he doesn't lose himself in the process.

Seven

CLAYTON

The Hayes family farm is on the outskirts of town, on the opposite end of Fontaine from Fire Creek. I park my car on the shoulder of the road just beyond the gate while I wait on Bennett to show up. Considering the location of the farm, I think it's a safe bet that it isn't a coincidence. Emmitt Hayes can't stand the sight of a Darcy and neither could his father.

Getting out of the car, I lean against the door and keep my gaze locked on the glimmer of headlights that I can catch through the trees. The gravel road up to the farm is one hairpin turn after another. It'll still be a solid five minutes before I actually see Bennett, even though he's probably not even a quarter of a mile from me.

I don't really know what I'm going to find, but whatever it is, I pray it's enough. I've given Samuel a heads-up about the tax issues. That was one of the biggest things I was holding over his head. I hope I won't have to regret that later.

Bennett's truck finally rolls up, and he gets out to punch in the access code at the gate. The chain link rolls slowly to one side and he looks back at me.

"Go ahead," he says. "But don't even think about walking up to that door without me. Emmitt's not a big fan of people with your last name."

"I know the feeling," I reply. The name Darcy isn't exactly an easy burden to bear. It comes with a lot of expectations and a lot of well-earned mistrust. I've been fighting it all my life, and now, with everything I've had to do to get what I need on Samuel, I feel sullied by it.

Thinking about Bennett's warning as I drive through the gate, I know there's no way in hell I'm getting out of that car to approach him first. Emmitt Hayes is roughly the size of a mountain and looks like he lives on raw, potentially protesting, meat. The last thing I want to do is give that big, crazy son of a bitch an excuse to take a bite out of me.

After we've both parked in front of the house, and Bennett has gotten out and climbed the steps to the door, I fall in behind him. He motions for me to stay back and I stop instantly. I don't consider myself a coward, but when facing down a savage animal, caution isn't exactly a bad idea.

Bennett knocks on the door. No answer. He knocks again. Nothing. He's lifting his hand, preparing to knock a third time, when the lights come on inside. Emmitt appears at the door. His dark hair is rumpled, he's sporting a beard that any *Duck Dynasty* fan would be proud of and he's wearing a pair of coveralls that, well, I don't want to think about what's on them. *Do not piss him off*, I tell myself.

"What the hell are you doing here?" he demands,

giving his younger brother a glare that would send most men running.

"What the hell were you doing in bed?" Bennett fires back, clearly unimpressed with the posturing of the grizzly in front of him.

"I worked last night," Emmitt replies. "Country vets don't keep city hours, jackass."

"Do you have the file on Darcy?" Bennett asks.

Emmitt looks past him and at me. From the way his eyes narrow and from the sneer visible even through the massive beard, it's pretty obvious he recognized me immediately. But he doesn't acknowledge me, just turns back to his little brother.

"What the fuck are you up to, Bennett?"

Bennett motions me forward and with more reluctance than I care to admit to, I climb the steps and get closer to a man who'd see me dead as soon as look at me.

"We all have one thing in common," Bennett explains. "Samuel Darcy has ruined the life of every person standing here."

Emmitt just looks at him, and I can feel the weight of his judgment. Standing there in a rumpled dress shirt, with my suit jacket still draped over the front seat, I am about as far apart from Emmitt Hayes and his dirty coveralls as another person could be.

"I doubt that," Emmitt says. "I'm not inviting a third-generation thief into my goddamn house, Bennett, and I'm sure as hell not giving him what we found."

Bennett curses softly, clearly exasperated with his brother. "Emmitt, just listen for a damned minute, would you?"

"One minute," Emmitt agrees. "Make it count."

Bennett looks back at me, and I know that this is my chance to make it count. If I don't lay it all on the line and tell the whole truth, Emmitt will not only kick my ass, but I'll miss out on the best chance I have of ending this mess and coming out on top. "Samuel ran Fire Creek into the ground. He borrowed against the company until it was so deep in the hole there was no getting it out. For years, he's been using it as his own private checking account...taking out money and never investing it back. We were on the brink of foreclosure when the three of us, Quentin, Mia, and I, took all that we had, pooled it, and bought sixty percent of the company outright. Right now, I'm looking for anything I can use to make Samuel sign over the remaining forty and the house."

"Your family problems are no concern of mine," Emmitt replies stiffly. "That whole damn place could burn to the ground and I wouldn't even blink."

I shrug. I've given it the best shot I have. "I never did anything to you, Emmitt. Not me. I've scoured every document in the archives. There's not a slip of paper that I haven't looked over to see if I could find a shred of proof that your great-grandfather had bought into Fire Creek. If it ever existed, it's gone now."

"Actually," Bennett interrupts. "It's not. We have it."

I shake my head. I can't quite believe what I'm hearing. I've been working like a damned fool looking for something and they've had it all along. "What? Why the hell haven't you done anything with it?"

"The man wants to destroy his family business. Let him," Emmitt answers. "We don't want it. The very idea of that place leaves a bad taste in my mouth. It destroyed our great-grandfather. Our grandfather lived like a beggar because of it, and our father died consumed with finding proof of it. I hate that damn place...and I don't have a lot of love for its occupants."

"Emmitt," Bennet says cautiously. "I trust him. If we give him this, it gets us all something we want."

"What's that?" Emmitt demands. He's clearly unimpressed with the conversation.

"Freedom," I reply. I don't know what it means to them, but to me, it means that I get my life back. I get to spend time with my wife and my daughter and not worry about prison sentences. It means I don't have to live every day prepared to kill my own father just to save the people I love from him. "It gets Samuel Darcy as far out of the picture as I can get him without digging him a grave. It gives Mia and Bennett a chance to make things right."

Emmitt looks at Bennett. I can't say he's softening. I don't know that word will ever be able to be applied to him. But there's less open hostility, and that's a good sign. "All this for that damned girl?" he asks.

"The *only* girl," Bennett answers, and there's not a shred of doubt or hesitation in his voice. "But also, it's the right thing to do. Trust me, Emmitt."

Emmitt makes a disgusted sound and slams the door in our faces. Maybe I'd counted my chickens too soon. Son of a bitch.

"That was an epic waste of time," I say, and turn back toward my car.

Bennett doesn't move, just stands there at the door. "Just wait."

Not even a full minute later, the door opens again, and Emmitt shoves a heavy file folder at Bennett. "Do what you want with it. I'm tired of that shit taking up space."

The door slams again, the lights go off, and we're left standing on the porch in the dark. I don't even know what the hell just happened.

I look up at Bennett, barely able to make him out in the pitch black. "Is he always like that?"

"No," Bennett replies smoothly. "He was actually in a pretty good mood tonight."

I'm shaking my head in amazement. Unable to really process what just happened. "So what is all that?" I ask, gesturing pointlessly in the dark toward the folder.

"Sworn affidavits, signed, witnessed, and notarized from the county clerk who was in office when, in 1962, your grandfather bribed him to make the original contract between him and our grandfather disappear. Your father was present," Bennett replies.

Holy fucking hell. They've been sitting on something that would have entitled them to strip Fire Creek right out of our hands and they've never made a move. What the hell else have they been sitting on?

"That's a thick folder for one document."

Bennett grins. In the darkness, I can just see the faint gleam of his too-white teeth. "That's only one thing your family did to ours. There's the property taxes that were only raised on our farm, courtesy of Samuel. There were the bank loans that would randomly come due because our payments weren't being applied to our loans. He held sway over this town because everyone here feared him. But they loved my father, and when he got sick, people came here of their own free will and gave him the evidence he'd been trying to gather his whole life."

It's everything I need and more. God above. And it's just being dropped into my hands. "Does Mia know about this?" I ask. It might piss her off. It might do a lot of things. She's been through so much in the last month that I'm not sure of just how clear her thinking is.

"Not yet," he replies softly. "I'll tell her...but she's had a rough day. He lied to her about your mom's accident. He told her Patricia wrecked because she was out looking for Mia."

I always wondered what he had on her, what sway Samuel used to bend her to his will. Now I know and I hate him even more. "While Mia was with you," I surmise. "Even if it were true, that's still not Mia's fault."

Bennett nods. "Well, that's what she's been living with for the last ten years...with him putting that in her head every chance he got."

I open the back door of the car and pull out the bag Evelyn had packed. "I don't know what's in there. I called Evelyn and she went back to the house and packed for her while I kicked Samuel's ass out."

Bennett grinned in the darkness. "I would have liked to see that."

"It was bloodless," I reply. Regrettably bloodless. I wish now that I'd at least taken a swing at him.

"Disappointing." The sad note in Bennett's voice tells me I'm not the only one who would have liked to see Samuel with his ass in the dirt and a couple of his perfect teeth missing.

I'd had to tip my hand pretty heavily to get him gone. I'd pretty much given him everything I had on him and provided him the chance to cover his tracks. It had been a strategic concession, and it would complicate things in the future. But with what Hayes had given me, I was still going to come out on top. If it allows Mia a chance at real peace and possibly even happiness, it will all be worth it. "I'll check in with Mia tomorrow. I'm sure she needs the rest."

"I will look after her," Bennett says. There's a tone in his voice, proprietary and a little defensive, like I'm doubting his intentions.

"If I doubted that for a minute, I would have thrown you out of the hospital myself two weeks ago," I remind him.

Bennett points to the folder. "Whatever you do with all that, make it count."

"He's broke...flat fucking broke," I confess. It feels good to say this shit to someone. "He's living on credit that's about to be maxed out and mooching off friends who haven't quite figured it out yet. This,"—I tap the file folder—"was the final piece to force his hand."

"Into what?"

I smile. It's so close I can taste it. "Leaving. There's a ratty condo in Boca Raton with his name on it. If he wants to live in the lap of luxury, he's going to have to start dating twenty years older instead of just twenty years old."

Bennett laughs out loud. "That, I would actually pay to see...but only the G-rated version. God above."

"Go take care of Mia," I tell him. Like I plan to go take care of Annalee. Tonight, it's time to confess. "I'll let you know how this shakes out."

Bennett nods and opens the door to his truck. When he does, a picture comes fluttering down from the visor. I stoop to pick it up but Bennett is already in his truck and gone. Getting into my car, I turn on the dome light and take a look at the photo.

"Son of a bitch!"

We've been searching for a link between Samuel and Katherine Shelby and it was right under our noses all along. A much younger Erica McCoy is staring back at me from the photo with her arm around her equally blonde and tanned friend, Katherine. It would be right up Samuel's alley to be screwing the best friend behind his mistress's back.

Conscious of being alone and unarmed on Emmitt Hayes's property, I don't stick around too long. I key the ignition and add the file and the photo to the box of evidence I've gathered. I've got a shit ton of work to do.

eight

ANNALEE

I've put Emma Grace to bed in Mia's room. She's got some clothes at Patricia's so it won't be too much of an issue to get her ready for school in the morning. Luckily, I'd had the foresight to bring her backpack with me so she wouldn't have to go to school sans homework in the morning.

I glance at the clock. It's pushing ten and I've still had no word from Clayton. I'm worried. The only thing predictable about Emmitt Hayes when it comes to a Darcy is hatred. And that's in public. For a Darcy to show up on his property, even in the company of his brother, is no guarantee. If Clayton comes in a bloodied mess, I'm going to have to raise fifteen kinds of hell.

I check on Patricia again. She's on a regular schedule with feedings, meds, turning and repositioning her. Everything has been done. I'm doing it more for my own peace of mind and to distract me from other worries than because she actually needs it.

I hear the back door open and I go to the kitchen to see Clayton walking in. He's carrying a heavy file box which he sets on the counter.

"You wanted my secrets," he says. "There they are. That's what I've been accumulating for the last year on Samuel. I've lied. Cheated. Bribed. I've had his apartment and office wired. That's all the dirt I uncovered. And tonight, Emmitt Hayes handed over a folder that makes this look like child's play."

I can't believe what I'm seeing. Half afraid, I pull the lid off the box and look inside. Photos of Samuel with women other than Erica are on top. There are copies of receipts and credit card statements attached to them. He's been using his company credit card to pay for hotel suites for trysts with women that are younger than his own daughter. I feel a little sick just looking at it.

"Why?" I ask him. "I don't understand. Why now?"

Clayton sits down at the kitchen island. There are dark circles under his eye. He looks tired and beaten down in a way I haven't seen before. I realize in that moment just how heavy a burden he's been carrying.

"In two months, Mama will receive the last payment from the trust her parents left. It was ten million dollars. There's another trust that'll mature in about five months and that has enough money to ensure that she has all the care she needs for the rest of her life...because we're broke, Annalee. All of us. Me, Quentin, Mia...we've sunk everything into Fire Creek, and he's bleeding it dry."

I didn't know any of this. He never hinted at money problems. Every month, like clockwork, he's put the same amount of money in the account I use for the household bills and he's done it without complaint.

"Clayton, why didn't you say something? I could have cut back...I could have gotten a job."

That pissed him off. I can see it instantly. I can see that muscle ticking in his jaw where he's clenched them so tight.

"That's not what I promised you," he says sharply. "I told you when you agreed to marry me that you'd never have to worry again, never have to scrimp and save and do without...not ever a-fucking-gain."

I'm shaking my head at him. Yes, he promised me that. And when Emma Grace was born, he said that it made him happy to know that I could stay home with her, that I could take care of our daughter and be the kind of mom I wanted to be. I never considered for a moment that he might be pushing himself too hard to make those things happen, that the cost to him might be greater than he'd ever realized.

I thought Clayton was being selfish and keeping his secrets. But the truth of the matter is, I've been selfish, too. I never asked. I never questioned. I never once stopped to think about what he might be giving up to give me what I wanted. From the moment I met him, Clayton has always been this upstanding guy. I never understood just what a feat that was until I met his father. His whole life has been spent trying to be what his father never could or would...a good man. And because of my own issues, because of my own fear that he might be hiding something worse than the fact that he had to bend a few rules to do right by all of us, I pushed him away. But he let me, and for some reason, that's harder to forgive than anything else.

"I'd rather scrimp and save and do without, I'd rather go back to working a crappy job, than to see you doing this to yourself...Clayton, you're killing yourself with all this. Do you not see that?"

"I was," he agrees. "But I'm done now. I've got what I

need, Annalee. Without Samuel draining every penny of profit we earn, we can make it work. The distillery is earning. Fire Creek is solid. It's just him."

I look back at the box and all the assorted papers. As I begin sifting through it, I see things that could not possibly have been obtained legally. Tapes, financial records, background checks. There are reports from private investigators. At the bottom of the box is a photo of Erica, Samuel's mistress who works at the distillery, and another woman, along with newspaper clippings about that woman drowning in the Kentucky River. It was never investigated as murder. The assumption, according to the newspaper, is that she'd fallen from an unidentified boat.

"Do you think Samuel was involved in this?"

"I know he was. I can't prove it, but I know it." His answer is firm, matter of fact. "That was Katherine...the older, perfect sister of the woman who Mia inadvertently hired to care for Mama but was snooping through the house instead. That picture of her and Erica together is circumstantial at best, but it's a link between Samuel and the dead woman, when we've never been able to make one before."

He stops for a minute, drawing in a deep breath. It's like the magnitude of what's just fallen into his lap is finally sinking in. He continued, "The Shelbys are all mixed up in this. Barbara, and Katherine's death, then Elizabeth turning up and nearly killing Mia. There's the letter Barbara Shelby wrote that Mia found, detailing her affair with Samuel...all laid out in a gloating confession that sent Mama running from the house in tears...the one that apparently led to Mama driving away and wrapping her car around a tree."

He says it dispassionately, but I know it bothers him. He was the one who cleaned out the car afterward, he picked up the scattered contents of her purse from the floorboard while staring at the bloodstained seat where she'd been cut from the car. I know that will haunt him forever.

"Do you think Samuel killed her?"

"I can't say. I think it was his boat she was on before she wound up in the water...but if she went in to the river by accident or not, he still left her there. He didn't alert anyone for help. He might not have killed her, but he didn't lift a hand to save her."

Something else catches my eye. It's a letter from an attorney addressed to Samuel. It's about the trust that was established by Patricia's parents and the final payment from it. It's only a couple of months away.

"So he wants the rest of Patricia's money," I surmise.

"Yes."

"When did you find out?" I demand.

"It was before Japan. The day I left," he admits. "That's what was on my mind while I was there...and when I came back. Trying to figure out what I needed to do about it, how to make it work. I only knew that I had to find some way to get him out of the picture, to keep Mama safe and make sure she didn't wind up in the kind of home he wanted to put her in from the beginning."

There is one thing that he said there that sticks out in my mind. *Get him out of the picture.* "How exactly were you going to get him out of the picture? What were you planning to do, Clayton?" I'm afraid of his answer. I'm afraid of just how far he would go if he thought it meant saving the rest of us.

"It's not what I wanted to do...but I was prepared,

Annalee, to end him if I had to. That's why—" He just stops, like he can't bring himself to say anymore.

"That's why what?" I demand. "You need to explain all of this, Clay, and you need to do it now." It's too much to take in. Looking at everything he's amassed, at all the planning and scheming, the digging and searching that he's done, I can't even fathom when he slept.

"That's why," he says softly, "when you asked for a divorce, I gave it to you. If I had to go down for killing the son of a bitch, I wasn't going to take you down with me."

I hit him. I can't help it. I punch him in the shoulder because it's the only part of him I can reach. It feels so good, I do it again. "You *stupid*, selfish, asshole! How dare you! How dare you make those kinds of decisions about my life, about our daughter's life, without even bothering to talk to me!"

He catches my hand when I swing at him again, not hurting me, but holding me so tightly I can't do anything but fume. "I had to," he says, and his voice is the merest whisper against my ear. "I had to keep you all safe, and I had to keep my promises to you...and to Emma Grace. I promised her when she was born that she would not grow up the way you did, that she would never feel forgotten, never feel like her mother wasn't there for her. Telling you anything about my plan would have made you an accessory...I was prepared to go to prison, Annalee, but I wasn't going to do it and leave our baby girl alone."

I'm so confused by what he's telling me, I can't even think straight. Part of me wants to kiss him, to hold onto him as tight as I can because whatever he might believe and however stupid he might have been, he's still the best man I've ever known. Another part of me wants to knock him in the head for being such an idiot.

"Let me go."

"Not if you're going to hit me again," he replies evenly. "I might deserve it but it's been a hell of a day and I just don't think I can take it."

"I'm not going to hit you." I won't. I may want to, but I won't. I'm going to attempt to be a rational adult.

He steps back, letting go of my hands and I turn to face him again. The way he's looking at me makes me squirm a little. "What?"

Shaking his head, he answers, "You said that if I gave you the truth before you signed the papers, we were good. Is that still true?"

I don't know. No, I do. But I'm not quite ready to say it yet. "Maybe. Probably. I've got to figure out if I can forgive you for being a dumbass man."

"I was a dumbass man when you married me," he points out.

"Slightly less dumb," I retort. "And I was too young and stupid to know it wasn't going to get any better."

He reaches for me, and this time when he takes my hand, it's not to keep me from hitting him. Instead, he presses my hand to his chest. I can feel the heat of him, the firm muscle beneath fabric and the steady thump of his heartbeat. "How about we both act young and dumb tonight? No promises. No talk of how things are going to play out. The future can work itself out...tonight, let's just do what feels good."

God, it's tempting. Like chocolate cake during PMS tempting. But I'm still hesitant. Scared, even. I can't let go of him again. The first time nearly broke me. "I don't know if that's a good idea."

"Doesn't have to be a good idea," he replies, and his hand has encircled my wrist, his thumb drawing lazy circles on sensitive skin until I shiver. "Just has to feel good. Tell me you don't want it...that you don't need it just as bad I do?"

I'm caving. Giving in even though I know I shouldn't. Yes, he's given me the truth, but that doesn't make everything just go away. There are issues to be talked about, decisions to be made. But for the night, I just want to let all that ride. I want him to make me forget how lonely I've felt for the last twelve months.

"Let's go upstairs," I whisper. I hate how breathless I sound, how needy and how fucking horny I so obviously sound. I'm either asthmatic or auditioning to do voice overs in porn.

He steps back. "I'll meet you in my old room. I've got to put all this stuff somewhere safe."

I watch him carry the box upstairs. Standing behind him, I take just a moment to enjoy the play of muscle, of long legs and a tight, firm ass. My mind is drifting to what it feels like to cup that perfect ass in my hands while he's driving into me. Yes, I am too fucking horny to make good decisions. My emotions might be mixed up and all over the place, but my physiology is pushing me in one very solid direction.

Listen to your body. That's the advice they give in every yoga class I've ever been to. Somehow, I don't think this is what they had in mind. Of course, they've never had the pleasure of having Clayton Darcy in their beds and I have. That man could tempt a saint.

Climbing the stairs, I make my way to Clayton's old room. Luckily, it's not an homage to his childhood. He'd moved back home for a while after Patricia's accident and had given it the adult makeover. The bed is small, a full-size, but I don't think that's going to be a problem for us.

I hear his footsteps in the hall. I reach for the hem of my shirt and tug it up and over my head. As he walks through the door, I toss it to him. He looks down in confusion for a second, then smiles before looking up at me.

If I'd had more time to plan, I'd be wearing sexier lingerie. But the way he's looking at me, it doesn't matter. My body responds instantly, my nipples hardening into taut points. The anticipation of having his hands on me, his mouth, it's too much. I can feel the wetness between my thighs.

Before I can say anything, he's already across the room and his arms are around me. He pulls me in close, his hands cupping my face. I love when he touches me this way. It makes me feel special...it makes me feel desired.

He kisses me and everything just falls away. All the hurt, the anger, the lingering doubts. I still think he fucked up, but the bottom line is I just don't care. He came back to me. He kept his promise.

His mouth is on mine. He's sucking and nipping at my lower lip until I moan. That moan is all the invitation he needs. His tongue slips inside, thrusting boldly into my mouth, mimicking what I know will come later. I press myself against him, eager for more, urging him on.

He doesn't seem to be in any great hurry. Sometimes that's a good thing, but after a year of having nothing between my thighs that wasn't battery operated, I'm a little impatient. I grasp the front placket of his shirt and pull. Buttons skitter, popping off and rolling over the floor to disappear between the furniture.

"What's the hurry?" he asks with a soft laugh.

If I don't say something outrageous, if I don't do something that makes him completely lose control, he will drag his feet and torture me like this all night.

"I can't wait, Clayton. I want your cock inside me." I don't know that I've ever, in the twelve years I've known him, said anything quite that crude to him. But it works. His eyes darken, the tension in him shifts into something darker. He's not holding back now.

He picks me up and spins me around until my back is pressed against the door. His hands are at my waist, unsnapping my jeans and lowering the zipper. But he doesn't push them off my hips, instead he just slips his hand inside, his fingers moving over the lace that is the only barrier between us. When his fingers slip beneath my panties, moving over bare skin, I can't hold back the moan.

"Clayton, just touch me...for the love of God, don't make me wait."

I don't have to ask him again. His hand dips lower, two fingers sliding inside me while his thumb brushes against my clit. My head falls back and I can't catch my breath. He's holding me there, my weight supported by his thighs, my legs draped over his, and he's driving me insane with just that touch. The need is like a living thing inside me, clawing and wild.

"You feel so good," he whispers hotly. "I can't wait to be inside you, to feel you closing around me. But first, I want to make you come. I want to make you remember just how good I can make you feel."

I can't respond. I can't even think. He knows just how to touch me to make me wild. I'm clutching at his shoulders, my nails sinking into his flesh as he takes me higher. I let out a broken sob that might have been a plea, or just some unintelligible muttering of his name. But abruptly, he stops.

I cry out in protest, but it's cut short as he turns and drops me on the bed. It bounces under me, but my focus is on him and the way he grabs my jeans and strips them off me. I part my thighs, instinctively welcoming him. His hands slide under me, around my thighs and he pulls me toward him, dipping his head to press a hot kiss against my inner thigh. Then he bites, his teeth scraping over my skin in a way that makes me shiver and moan.

"Clayton, you're killing me! Please!"

I don't care that I'm begging. I'll plead. I'll cry. I'll do whatever it takes to escape this knife edge of need.

Nine

CLAYTON

I can't even count the number of nights I've lain awake dreaming of her like this. Cold showers, jacking off like a horny teenager, nothing helped. There were moments where I was even tempted to find another woman just to chase away her ghost. But those thoughts were always quickly dismissed, mostly because I knew no other woman would ever do, and because I knew that whatever it took, someday I'd have her back...I'd have her laid out before me just like this.

Touching the silken skin of her thighs, inhaling the hot, drugging scent of her, I dip my head again, but it isn't her thigh I kiss. Instead, I press my lips against the slick folds of her sex, sliding my tongue between them and tasting her. She moans and shivers beneath me, so I repeat the gesture, this time licking all the way up to the hardened nub of her clit.

She grabs my hair, her fingers tightening in it to the point of pain as she arches beneath me. I suck her clit into my mouth and she goes quiet. Annalee was never a screamer. When she's close, hovering on the edge of orgasm, she holds her breath and not a sound escapes her. I slip two fingers inside her, curling them forward as I withdraw, all the while keeping my mouth on her clit. I know what she likes. I've always known. There's power in that, but it's a two-way street. She can make me beg, too.

Her whole body trembles, from head to toe, every muscle tightening, and then going lax. I can feel the pulse of her orgasm on my tongue. Her grip on my hair loosens, and she simply sinks into the bed, all the tension leaving her.

"Oh god," she breathes. "I forgot how good that could feel."

"We're not done yet. Not by a long shot," I tell her.

Immediately she sits up on the edge of the bed and reaches for the fly of my pants. Her lips are curved in a seductive smile as she frees the button and lowers the zipper. "You are so right about that."

I kick off my shoes and push my pants down. I don't know what she has in mind, but as long as it involves both of us getting to come at some point, I don't care. She slides off the bed onto the floor until she's on her knees in front of me. I can feel her breath on my cock, the hard points of her nipples pressed against my thighs.

She leans in and kisses the head of my cock, her tongue swirling over me like it's a treat, it's all I can do not to lose it right there. I don't doubt for a minute that she knows exactly what she's doing to me. She's watching me watch her and putting on a hell of a show.

When she takes me in completely, sucking deep and hard, my breath hisses out. My hands are in her hair, whether to hold her there or push her away, I'm not sure.

It feels too good, and if she keeps going, this night is going to be a hell of a lot shorter than I planned.

"*Fuck*." The word comes out on a hiss as her hand closes tightly around me, sliding over me as she withdraws. "No more, Annalee. I can't take it."

She pouts, her full lips wet and glistening, hovering over me. "But I love doing this for you...I like making you moan."

"Some other time," I tell her and lift her onto the bed. I shed the rest of my clothes before joining her. Her thighs part immediately, her legs locking around me, guiding me home.

Sliding into the scorching heat of her, feeling her close around me like a fist, takes my breath away. Literally. With my weight resting on my elbows, looking down at her beautiful face—eyes closed, her lips parted on a soft cry—I never thought I'd have this again.

Nudging a little deeper, I take one hand and slide it behind her knee, hiking it up just a little further. I swear to God, she could probably hook her foot behind her own head. I've never been so happy to have paid for yoga classes in my damned life.

The angle is perfect. I knew it would be because I know her, her body, every little tell, every place to touch her that makes her shiver and moan. Her stomach is quivering, the muscles flexing and contracting rhythmically. I can feel the tension in her thighs before the first stroke.

She opens her eyes and looks at me. A smile spreads across her lips, slow and sexy. Her hair is fanned out on the pillow and there's a soft flush on her cheeks...she's every fantasy I've ever had and I'm balls deep inside her right now. For the first time in a goddamn year, my life is nearly perfect.

"What are you waiting for, Clay? You've got me where you want me...do something about it," she dares.

I flex my hips against hers, deeper, thrusting just a little. "Once I start, it'll be a mad rush to the finish line. I want this moment to savor."

She moves against me, her hips undulating in a slow circle that it takes everything in me to resist. I place one hand on her hips, holding her still. She's not taking control. Not this time anyway.

"I like looking at you this way—watching your eyes flutter closed when you moan my name, watching your lips part when you cry out." I pause for a second and then utter words that I know will make her crazy. "And knowing that every time you moan, beg or call out to God, it's because I've got my cock buried inside the sweetest pussy I've ever tasted." She shudders beneath me, her whole body reacting to the statement like it was something physical.

Her hands fist in the bedclothes and she strains against me, arching upward and taking me in just a little deeper. I have to grit my teeth and count just not to come on the spot.

I withdraw almost completely, feeling her body clench around me, trying to hold on. I'm not gentle when I plunge into her again. It's hard and fast, even a little angry. Her hands are on my back, her nails digging into my shoulders, and she throws her head back on a sob.

I grab her wrists and pin her hands to the bed with mine. The little bit of control I had is now long gone. There's no sound in the room except our heavy breathing and our bodies coming together.

It's no longer about finesse or skill. It's just need and the animalistic drive to finish, to mark her, to make sure that she and everyone else know she's mine.

The heat of her closes around me, her inner muscles flexing and clenching in a rhythm that makes my head spin. Every thrust and withdrawal, I'm aware of her, of the tension in her thighs, the quivering of her belly. When I feel her hips arch beneath me, her body pushing up from the bed as her head falls back, her lips part on a silent cry. I can feel the pulsing of her body around me as she comes for me.

I'm right behind her. Driving deep one last time, I press my face against her neck and let it wash through me.

ANNALEE

Clayton's weight presses me down into the bed, his hands are still shackling my wrists. I've never felt trapped by him. Only cherished, protected, desired. It's no different now, except that I had forgotten just how good it feels to have him inside me, to feel the strength and heat of him. I've also forgotten how good it feels to orgasm with someone else, no batteries required.

He shifts slightly, withdrawing from me. I shiver at the movement. All the nerve endings are still firing, creating a heightened sensitivity to every touch. I'm still waiting for the world to right itself. Yes, the sex was amazing. It always was. That was why it was such a blow when he just stopped touching me, stopped looking at me, when I'd go to bed and wake up alone. I didn't understand the shift, and a part of me still doesn't.

"This doesn't mean we're back together," I say aloud. It would be more convincing if my breath wasn't still ragged and my voice didn't sound like, well, like I'd just been fucked.

"Can we fight later? I'm too tired now," he replies.

"Asshole."

He rolls off me completely, onto his back to stare up at the ceiling. "I don't think we *can* go back to where we were, instantly. But do you think we can at least wait until our heart rates have returned to normal before we're at each other's throats again?"

I turn on my side. "Is that what this is? At each other's throats? I thought we were having a conversation."

"We can't have a conversation...not until all the blood makes it back to my brain anyway."

He's got me there. There's no denying that, at least at the present moment, I have the advantage. "What are you going to do now...about Samuel?"

He scratches his chest. I watch his hand moving over his skin, mesmerized by it. I've had two mind-blowing orgasms. It shouldn't be possible to want more, but I do.

"First thing tomorrow, I meet with the attorney and get the papers drawn up that will allow him to transfer guardianship to Mia, Quentin, and myself. Then the house...Quentin doesn't want it. He can barely stand to step foot in it. I don't know if Mia does or not, but my plan is to have him deed it to her."

"And the evidence in the box? That's all just to make him go along with it? Nothing happens to him for committing heaven only knows how many crimes?"

"I'm going to do what I can. But if it comes down to getting justice or just ensuring that the people I love are taken care of, you know what I have to go with. All of this was for Mama...and for you, Emma Grace, Mia. He's destroyed too many people already," Clayton says. The hand that was on his chest has moved over and is now tracing lazy circles on my hip.

"Stop trying to distract me. How do you get that evidence to someone to do something with it and not incriminate yourself?"

"I can't," he admits. "I could maybe give Matt Crawford a heads up about some of it, but the really serious stuff is out of his jurisdiction."

"Do what you need and then just let it all go...I don't care if he goes to prison. I don't care what happens to him as long as I get to have you back."

He looks at me. "I thought this didn't mean we were back together."

"Don't be an idiot. Of course we'll get back together. But we need to, on the surface, take things slow. Emma Grace is already confused enough."

Clayton laughs. "She isn't confused about anything. That kid has it more put together than either one of us."

I can't deny that. "Fine. *I'm* confused. Happy?"

He smiles at me, tugs me closer until I'm tucked against his side. "I'm getting there. If you let me get some sleep now, we could probably do this again before I have to leave in the morning."

I reach behind me and turn off the lights. "Fine. But if it's early morning, you're doing all the work."

"Yes, ma'am."

Ten

CLAYTON

I'm sitting in my office with my attorney. John has known what I had in mind for a long time now, so when I called him to ask for the documents, he brought them over along with a celebratory six-pack.

"You do realize it's only ten in the morning?" I ask him.

"You're about to hand your crooked SOB of a father his proverbial ass, and your wife's attorney called me this morning to call a halt to divorce proceedings...not cancel them, just put a hold. Still, I figure that means you wormed your way back into her good graces. If that doesn't call for celebration, what does?"

I grab one of the beers and pop it open. "You make an excellent point."

John pulls a folder from his briefcase and places it on my desk. "That's everything you asked for. Transfer of guardianship, a deed of transfer for the house, and a deed of transfer for the remaining forty percent of Fire Creek.

Get his signature, I'll file everything with the clerk and then that son of a bitch can fall off the face of the earth."

I frown. "I know why I hate him...but why do you?"

"I've handled a lot of divorces in this town," John admits. "And he comes up...again and again and again. Let's just say that I knew long before you showed up at my door that he was poison."

I nod and take a sip of my beer. Day-drinking at the office is probably not the smartest thing I've ever done, but I'm still riding on a high. Waking up with Annalee wrapped around me was one of those perfect moments that you just want to hang on to.

"So when does this all go down?"

I check my watch. "I've got about ten minutes before he strolls in."

John takes his beer and chugs it before getting to his feet. "In that case, I'll see you around. I don't want to be anywhere in the vicinity when that shitstorm happens."

"Coward," I say with a grin.

"Damn straight," John agrees and heads for the door.

As he leaves, I look through the paperwork to make sure everything is in order. It's all falling into place, but Samuel Darcy is no one's fool. I can have everything in place, but that doesn't mean he won't still manage to weasel his way out of it.

With a few minutes to spare before he shows up, I take my phone from my jacket pocket and send a text to Annalee.

Keep thinking about how you looked this morning. Naked. In my bed.

I turn to the window and watch the parking lot, waiting for my first glimpse of Samuel's car, but the second my phone buzzes, I'm checking to see what she said. Please, let it be dirty.

I'm standing in MY walk-in closet trying to decide if you're worth giving up half the space for.

I can't help but smile at her reply, even as I'm tapping out my own.

We could just give up clothes altogether. I'm a big fan of nudity where you're concerned.

Samuel's car pulls in. Play time is definitely over. I leave my phone on the desk and grab the forms that John dropped off along with my laundry list of my father's sins. He won't go quietly. But he'll go. Whatever it takes.

I'm sitting in his office when he walks in. The sneer on his face is telling. He's still ticked at being outmaneuvered last night, which means that this is really going to set off a bomb.

"You're in the wrong office," he says. "You don't get this one till I die."

"I'll get it a little sooner than that," I reply. "You should sit down. You're not going to like this conversation very much."

He tosses his briefcase onto the desk and takes off his jacket before walking to the antique breakfront cabinet that has been in there since the beginning of time. He pours himself a healthy dose of some of our best bourbon. I'm not really surprised when he doesn't offer me one, not that I'm interested in having a drink with the old man anyway. I'll do my drinking when he's finally gone for good.

"Get on with it then," he says. "More extortion and blackmail from my eldest son?"

"Am I? Your eldest? I know Quentin and I aren't your only sons, or so rumor would have it."

"My eldest legitimate son," he corrects. "You shouldn't be so quick to acknowledge the bastards. They'll only try to take a piece of what's yours."

113

I'm shaking my head. It's a typical response for him, always putting himself first. Greed and avarice are the things he understands. The idea that I could have brothers and sisters out there I don't know leaves me with a sick feeling in my gut. But all he cares about is the cost of acknowledging them.

"Without you digging your fingers into the pot to lavish gifts on yourself and your gold-digging, side-side bitches, we should have plenty to go around," I reply. "And for the record, that all stops today. Today, you're leaving Fontaine, Mama, the house, the distillery...today will be the last time any of us have to deal with your worthless ass."

Samuel laughs as if he's actually amused by this. "Son, you greatly mistake the amount of power you have here."

It's my turn to be amused. "Oh, it's not my power, Samuel. It's the power of the truth...and there's a little matter of evidence. I know all about how you and your worthless father cheated the Hayes family out of Fire Creek. Not only do I know about it, I have documentation."

He's not smiling now. "It'd never hold up in court. I'm the only person in that room who's still living."

"Yes, but the president of First Bank of Fontaine is still living. He had some pretty interesting things to say about how you coerced, bribed and intimidated his employees into holding the Hayes' mortgage payments instead of applying them to their account. Then there's the tax issue...or ten. You forcing other people's property taxes to be raised while the taxes on Fire Creek and the house mysteriously dropped."

"Is this what your sister whored herself to Bennett Hayes for?"

I want to punch him right in the damn mouth, but

losing my cool will only give him the upper hand. "Call her that again and I will gut you like a fish. I have this information for the simple fact that everyone in this town would happily watch you burn."

"I'm not giving you any of this...not the house, not the business, and you're sure as hell not getting guardianship over your mother."

I lean back in the chair and prop my feet on the desk. "I didn't put two and two together initially, but then after that little fiasco the other night, it all started to make sense."

"Get to the damn point, Clayton. You're trying my patience."

"I'm referring to the accidental drowning of Katherine Shelby. Was it...accidental that is?"

He scoffs, but I can tell he's on the run now. The nerves are starting to rattle. I can see it in him as he paces to the window and looks out. "I didn't hurt that girl. You're reaching."

"She fell off your boat, and you didn't do a goddamn thing to save her. That's an important distinction that the police have never been able to make. Her body washed up, but no one could say definitively where she'd come from. But I can."

"No, you can't! You don't know a goddamn thing!" he shouts.

"Let's just get Erica in here and ask her," I suggest. "It was that pic Bennett had snagged off Erica's social media that really sealed the deal there. The two of them were thick as thieves apparently."

"You leave Erica out of this," he says.

He doesn't give a damn about Erica. I know that, and so does he. But that answers another question I had. Erica and Katherine hadn't been on the boat together. Samuel

115

had been up to his same old tricks, wooing one behind the other's back.

"It'll go one of two ways...either Erica was on the boat with you and will tearfully confess, or she had no clue that you'd taken her best friend out that day without her. Which of those things is going to get you in the most trouble? That you were fucking her best friend or that you killed her?"

"You want the house and the distillery, you can have them both. But I refuse to turn guardianship of Patricia over to you or anyone else!"

"Guardianship isn't really what's holding you back." He's sweating now. I can see it. He needs Erica because she knows too much. She's also the missing piece that can incriminate him in what would amount to manslaughter, at the very least. "It's that final payment from the trusts that's keeping you here."

He punches the wall, a large hole appearing in the drywall next to the door. "Goddamn you and your snooping! Going through my trash, through my mail? What the hell kind of man did I raise?"

I meet his glare dead on. "You didn't raise anyone, male or otherwise. Patricia raised us and she did a damned fine job of it without you 'round...I'm willing to give you two things. You can have the condo in Boca Raton and when the trust comes through, I will give you one million dollars. Or, you can fight me on this and I can challenge your guardianship in court...and win, since you clearly don't have Mother's best interests at heart and never have. I can turn over all the evidence I have to the police about your wrongdoings and let them sort it out."

"You wouldn't dare!" He's shouting again, his face purple with rage.

"I would and I will. Maybe they can't charge you with

anything, but you'd be done for in Kentucky. Every door would be closed to you. The society, the parties, the clubs...you'd be shut out like a pariah."

"You are not doing this to me! You're not taking everything I've built—"

"You haven't built *anything*." I'm shouting now too, less out of anger than to be heard overtop his bellyaching. "You're bankrupting us and it's going to stop one way or another. Sign the fucking forms, Samuel, or I will make your life such a living hell, you'll pray for it to end."

I tap the forms on the desk with the pen. "Sign them and you get one million dollars and the opportunity to live out the rest of your life in a sunshiny paradise. Don't, and you face financial ruin, social ruin, and possibly prison. It's not a hard choice."

He snatches the pen and begins signing the documents by all the numerous flags attached to them. "I will make you regret this."

I don't say anything else. I don't need to. For the moment, I've won.

ANNALEE

In between Clayton's many flirty and dirty text messages, I've cleaned house all day. It's a coping mechanism. When I need to clear my head, I clean. Of course, I also need to make room for Clayton to move back in. Even though I've given him a hard time and told him it can't happen immediately, it won't be long. Once we talk to Emma Grace, it's pretty much a done deal. I smile thinking of how excited she'll be to have her daddy back home.

The exhaustion, as I head downstairs, isn't just about the work I've done today. It's about the fact I got no sleep last night courtesy of Clayton. Thinking about it, about him, and the way it felt to wake up in the middle of the night to the feeling of his hands on me, his mouth, I literally have to squeeze my thighs together. I feel hot immediately. It shouldn't be possible to want him again, but I do. The drought is officially ended. Thank God.

I glance at the clock. "Shit." I've got to get Emma Grace from school and get her to dance class. Even if I leave right now, I'm still going to be late. I grab my keys from the counter and head into the garage.

The instant I'm behind the wheel I know something is wrong. The seat has been moved. I glance at the rearview mirror and my stomach drops. Samuel is sitting in the back seat. I don't even have time to scream before he's got his hands over my mouth.

The chemical smell is overwhelming. My brain begins to fog immediately. I lay on the horn, but from inside the garage, with the door closed, no one will hear. I'm reaching for the garage door opener, but I can't lift my arm. It's too heavy. My vision wavers, growing dimmer. Oh god, no.

eleven

CLAYTON

I pull into the driveway that runs alongside Bennett's home. It's small, but it's a pretty enough place. Annalee would refer to it as quaint or having cottage charm. I'm shaking my head as I get out of the car. I can't stop thinking about her. It's as bad as it was when we first met.

Standing there in the gravel beside the porch, I hear the hum of power tools and follow the noise. Bennett is working in the converted barn behind the house. He looks up as I wander in, and finishes cutting the piece he's working on before turning off the machine.

In the center of the workroom is an old grand piano. It's been painted dark blue with enough of the wood still showing through to make it interesting. It's perched upright and the innards are gone, having been replaced with shelves.

"That's a cool piece," I say.

"You and Samuel have your showdown yet?" he asks.

Definitely to the point. "Yes. And it's done. He signed over everything...I want to talk to you about Mia, and about a few other things."

He nods and removes the safety goggles he's wearing.

"You seriously wear that shit when you're working?" I ask him.

"Ever had a splinter in your eye?" he fires back.

Fuck. I'm wincing just thinking about it. "No."

"Well, shove a piece of wood in your eyeball and then get back to me on whether or not goggles are a good idea."

I shudder. "Thanks, but I'll pass. I've been tortured enough for one day." I pull the deed to the house from my jacket pocket. "That's for Mia."

"You're not going to see her?"

I shake my head. "Not today. You all need to talk about that, decide how you want to handle it. If I'm in there, Mia's just going to want to talk about Samuel...and I'm kinda done with that topic for today."

"But he's gone?" Bennett asks. "He signed over everything and he's gone?"

"Going. Not sure when he'll get the hell out of Dodge, but it won't be long," I say. I shove my hands in my pocket and lean back against the door frame of the barn. "Do you really love her, or do you just love the idea of her after all these years?"

He cocks his brow and I can tell the question pissed him off. "It's not really your business...that's between Mia and me."

I walk forward until we're nose to nose. "I'm not here to bust your balls or to talk you out of being with her... but it's not a stretch to think that ten years apart is a long time, Bennett. People change. People grow the hell up in that length of time. Don't rush her, and don't let her rush you."

I turn to walk away but he stops me. "I do love her. Doesn't matter if it's been ten years or a hundred."

"Then taking it slow for the next few months won't matter that much, will it?"

He flips me the bird. In this fucked up, weird ass, almost family situation, I take that as a yes and get back in my car as I watch Bennett disappear inside the house. He'll be good to Mia and he'll be good for her, I don't have any doubts. But after so long, they need to take their time and not rush it. Second chances work but if they require a third, all bets are off.

I put my car into reverse and back out of the driveway, just as Carter Hayes pulls up in the rust pile he calls a truck. He rolls his window down which means he wants to talk. Pushing the button to lower mine, I look up at him. And that's why men drive trucks, I realize. I'm pissed off at having to look up at him.

"I've been working in your neighborhood a lot lately and I know this is the time of day your wife always goes to pick up the kid," he says. "And it might not be anything, but your daddy's car is parked just a block down from your house, and I didn't see your wife leave."

It's like my blood turned to ice in my veins. I feel cold all the way through. "Ask Mia to go get Emma Grace and bring her back here."

Carter nods and pulls past me to turn into the driveway, and I take off in a hail of flying gravel and dust. I've got to get to Annalee, and I can only pray I won't be too late.

121

ANNALEE

Someone is pounding rocks inside my skull. Opening my eyes, everything is blurry. I'm in my kitchen, in a chair beside the island, that much I know, but I'm seeing double of everything.

"I was really hoping you wouldn't wake up."

It's Samuel's voice. The fear is instant, spiking my heart rate and my blood pressure, which in turn makes the headache worse.

"What are you doing?" I ask. My voice sounds thick, the words slurred and barely intelligible.

"I drugged you. I helped myself to some of the gas that our local vet uses to anesthetize horses," he says, almost apologetically.

"Emmitt Hayes let you on his property?"

Samuel laughs. "Of course not. I got him preoccupied with a stray dog that someone, namely me, dumped at his gate after being run over by a car."

He'd run over a dog to create a distraction? Fuck. I try to sit up straighter in the chair, but I can't. I realize that my hands and feet are tied together, forcing me to slump forward.

"Why are you doing this?"

"You don't have to distract me or stall me...I don't plan to kill you until Clayton shows up," he explains, holding up the revolver and waving it like a madman. "I know better than to trust him, especially after today. Today, I saw just how much my son was like me."

Oh god. It's all starting to come together or the fog from the fucking horse tranquilizer he drugged me with is starting to lift.

"Samuel, I know you're angry at Clayton, but you

have to see that this won't work! If you do this, you'll go to prison!"

"I'll wind up there anyway," he says. "I can't trust him not to take what he has on me to the cops. We both know that he'd love nothing better than to see me suffer."

"Clayton keeps his word...always." And I'm going to pay the price for it. It's not fair to blame him. I know that. And as much as I love him, right now, he isn't what's on my mind. It's Emma Grace. She's sitting at her dance class, decked out from head to toe in her pink dance gear, staring longingly at the older girls who already get to wear toe shoes. What will this do to her? If this crazy son of a bitch actually puts a bullet in me, what on earth will happen to my baby girl?

"He's a real Boy Scout with all his spying, stealing, bribery," Samuel says bitterly. "The minute my back is turned, he'll burn me...but not if I burn him first."

"I don't know what that means." I am stalling, buying as much time as I can. Maybe he doesn't plan on killing me till Clayton walks in to see it, but the son of a bitch is crazy and could change his mind at any time. Clearly, he's cracked.

Samuel gets up from the table and starts pacing the kitchen, randomly looking in cabinets and drawers. "It means that my dear son will have a mental breakdown, shooting you, his estranged wife, and his divorce attorney, before setting the house on fire and putting a bullet in his own head."

I can feel the tears building, trying to break through. I can't let them. If I fall apart now, there's no getting out of it. Hell, there's no getting out of it anyway, but at least I won't give the bastard the satisfaction of seeing me cry.

"What about Emma Grace? Do you really want to leave your only grandchild without either of her parents?"

It's a reasonable question, something that would make most people pause at least. With him, I know it's a long shot.

"There's always collateral damage, Annalee...just be thankful she's not here to burn with you all," he replies. Both his tone and his eyes are completely cold. He's never been especially warm. Even when Samuel is being pleasant, there's been a vague sense of unease in his presence. I thought he was simply a narcissist. I was wrong. He's a full-blown sociopath.

There won't be any reasoning with him. I can't reach him because there's nothing inside. He's just a black hole, incapable of feeling. The only things he understands are power and destruction.

I don't really have a plan yet, only the faintest stirrings of one. But I have to get my hands free, otherwise, I'm going to die here and so will Clayton when he shows up. And he will. Because he is the Boy Scout Samuel accused him of being. When the dance teacher can't find me, she'll call him and then he will worry. I feel sick just thinking about.

"Can you please untie my hands for a moment? Just enough to let me sit up straight?" I plead with him, exaggerating the slurred speech. My head is starting to clear, but he doesn't need to know that. If he thinks I'm still loopy from the drugs, he might be a little less cautious. If I can just get my hands free, I might have a chance.

"No."

Of course, he's got to be a dick. Then again, I'm tied to a chair, him being a dick is kind of a given. "Please...it's the drug. I feel like I'm going to throw up! Sitting up will help."

He sighs. "I won't kill you until he's here, Annalee,

but that doesn't mean I won't hurt you. Don't try anything."

"I won't," I lie.

He lays the gun down on the counter and walks toward me. The ropes are tied in such a way that he has to crouch beside the chair to loosen them. The second my hands are free, I grab his hair and slam his face against the island. He hits it with a satisfying thud.

I'm stronger than I look and a hell of a lot stronger than he expected me to be. Once won't be nearly enough, but I've lost the element of surprise. It's not nearly as easy the second time, still I manage to bang his head against the wood one more time. He pushes me off, the chair tipping over.

Even though it hurt like a bitch, it was just what I needed. That allows me to slide my feet, and the ropes he'd used to tie them, over the legs of the chair. I'm free. Well, other than being trapped in the house with my murderous father-in-law, but at least for the moment I have the use of all my limbs.

I'm backing away from the island, barely on my feet before he's coming at me. Samuel is a big man, tall and broad-shouldered just like Clayton. All the yoga and Pilates in the world isn't going to make me strong enough to tangle with him. But I've got pretty good aim.

There's a shelf beside me that has all of our pretty and utterly useless dishes on it. They're finally going to get used for something, at least. One by one, I send those plates sailing at him. He manages to duck most of them, but he's not entirely unscathed. There's a cut over his eyebrow. It's going to scar. It's a little twisted just how happy that thought makes me.

The flying dinner plates have bought me enough time to get around the island. I grab one of the knives from the block. The gun is still too far away. He'll catch me before I can even get close to it.

"You can't win this, Annalee. There's no way you can stop me," he says smugly.

I don't have to stop him. Just slow him down. Clayton will be here. That's the thing I keep telling myself. Somehow, someway, he will show up because I need him to.

It's the last thought I have before Samuel charges me. I grip the knife tighter and wait for the impact.

Twelve

CLAYTON

I ease my car onto the driveway at the house. The garage door is closed, Annalee is nowhere in sight, but Samuel's car is still parked just down the street. I owe Carter Hayes. I owe him big.

Opening the garage door would be too loud. I have no idea what Samuel is up to but I know it can't be good. *Please, do not let me be too late.*

I move around to the side of the house. Emma Grace has a bad habit of opening the dining room doors and stepping out onto the deck without locking them back. I'm praying that I'm in luck and she's left them unlatched this time.

As I approach the door, I hear the sounds coming from inside. Shouting, breaking dishes—I've got to get in there. I try the door, and for once, it's actually locked. Son of a bitch. Breaking the glass is pretty much my only option.

I take off my jacket and put it against the pane before

putting my fist through it. There are a few minor cuts, but nothing so bad that it'll prevent me from knocking Samuel on his ass.

Once inside, I move past the table and to the kitchen door. What I see makes my blood run cold. Annalee is on the floor, Samuel is standing above her with a knife in his hands. They're both covered in blood, but whether it's his or hers, I have no idea.

I don't hesitate. I can't afford to. Without a second thought, I rush at Samuel, putting my shoulder right into his gut and taking him down. We're sliding across the kitchen floor until we land against the cabinet with a loud thud. More dishes crash and break. There's glass everywhere.

I feel the knife slicing at my shoulder, but it's a total disconnect. Whatever happens, he needs to be subdued before he can hurt her any more. I manage to pin him to the ground. I draw my fist back to hit him.

The sound of it, when his nose crunches beneath my fist, is oddly satisfying, so I hit him again. And again. I don't know how many times. All I know is that I can hear Annalee screaming behind me and my knuckles are raw and bloody by the time I'm finally coherent enough to stop.

I look down at Samuel. He's barely conscious and his face is a bloody mess. The knife is on the floor, his hands long since slack. I get to my feet slowly. The blood is rushing still, but that first wave of adrenaline has given way to just gut-clenching fear.

I kick the knife away and turn to Annalee. She's holding her arm, and I can see the blood seeping through her fingers, but she's got a gun in her hands.

"I called 9-1-1," she says. "They're sending paramedics and the sheriff. Where's Emma Grace?"

"Mia has her. She's safe." Even as I'm answering her, I'm grabbing a towel from the drawer and walking toward her. "Let me see."

"It's not bad," she replies stiffly.

Which means it is. "Let me see," I tell her again.

Reluctantly, she moves her hand, and I can see the deep gash in her forearm. There are others—little nicks and cuts on her hands and one on her cheek. Whether they're from the knife or from the broken glass everywhere, I have no idea. I wrap the towel around her arm and put pressure on it. "I should have fucking killed him."

ANNALEE

I've never seen Clay like this. He's not a violent man, but I truly thought he would kill Samuel. The fury that consumed him then is something I honestly didn't know he had inside him. I know he's scared for me, and I know how much he hates Samuel, but it's frightening to see this side of him. "He'll go to prison for this. We're done with him, Clayton. This is the end of it."

"I should have known," he whispers. "I should have realized this morning that he gave in too easy and that he was going to try something...but I never would have imagined this. I'm so sorry he hurt you."

There he is taking responsibility for everything again. "You can't control him or what he does. That isn't your job. I'm fine. Really. Just a scratch."

He gives me a look that is clearly skeptical. "That isn't a scratch. It's a fucking stab wound, Annalee. Because my father is a sociopath."

129

I lean against him. Oddly enough, it isn't because I need reassurance, but because he does. "Yes, he is. He's also nuttier than a ten-pound fruitcake, but currently he's unconscious because you beat the ever-loving shit out of him, so we're okay right now."

"Are we?" From his tone, I know he's not just talking about the crazy that just went down with Samuel. He's asking about something else altogether.

I roll my eyes at him even as I hear the approaching sirens outside. "Don't go fishing just yet."

The cops are coming in, the paramedics on their heels. I'm being bandaged up. Clayton's being questioned. I'm being questioned. Samuel's worthless carcass is loaded onto a gurney and wheeled away to the waiting ambulance.

Oh, the gossips of Fontaine are going to love this. I sense a vacation coming on. We can leave town and let them get all the talk out of their system before we come back. Except we're broke, I remind myself. Or, rather, we're the Darcy definition of broke, which is probably very different from mine. My childhood consisted of eating old peanut butter off the spoon because we were too poor to buy bread. There are definitely degrees of poor, and we're nowhere near the real shit.

"You're going to have to run that by me again, ma'am."

I meet the sheriff's dubious gaze. "He came here to kill me. But he didn't want to kill me until Clayton was here to witness it. He also planned to murder Clayton and his attorney and make the whole thing look like a murder-murder-suicide...because he's a nutball. I can't tell you why he's a nutball, Sheriff. That's beyond my scope of practice as a stay-at-home mother!"

The sheriff sighs, as if he's the one having a shit day. "You said he drugged you with horse tranquilizers?"

He sounds like maybe he thinks that's a good idea. "Yes. He said he stole them from Emmitt Hayes. He ran over a dog and dumped it at Emmitt's to create a distraction and then stole some kind of sedative gas."

"Sick bastard."

"*Really*? The *dog* is what gets you? Not the fact that he was going to leave my child an orphan?"

The sheriff's face flushes and he looks uncomfortable for a minute. "I think we've got enough, but if we have more questions, we'll be in touch."

I realize that rolling my eyes at local law enforcement is probably not helpful, but sometimes you just have to go with it. "Oh, I never doubted it."

The paramedics informed me earlier that I'd need stitches, which means a trip to the ER. I'm not crazy about it. As the house empties, leaving just Clayton and me standing in the shambles of it, I can actually take in the destruction of it all.

"I think I used every wedding gift we ever received as ammunition against your father," I say.

He smiles. "Isn't that the first time we've used most of them at all?"

I look at the broken glass everywhere. "And clearly the last."

"Let's go," he says. "I need to get you to the ER. And me too. I got stabbed in the shoulder apparently. Somehow, I missed that."

"Tends to happen when you go all 'Hulk smash' on someone."

He laughs and it's such a sweet sound after the craziness of the last few hours. "You're one to talk. You single-handedly destroyed this kitchen and kicked Samuel's ass, not to mention giving him a nice little stab wound. According to the paramedics, if you'd been half an inch to the right, he'd be a dead man. You are officially a badass."

"Only a little badass," I protest. I got in a few good licks, but I know that if Clayton hadn't shown up when he did, the outcome would have been very different. Samuel was surprised by the fact that I fought back. If I hadn't caught him off guard—well, I'm not going to think about that. I'm going to go get stitches in my arm and if we make it out of the ER before midnight, I'm going to Bennett's, I'm picking up my baby girl, and I'm going to try to put this insanity behind us.

Looking around the kitchen, I shake my head. "I can't bring Emma Grace home to this mess."

"It's taken care of," he says. "I called Evelyn. She's coming over to sweep up the mess. And once it's done, Mia's bringing Emma Grace back home and settling her into her own bed for the night. She'll be here waiting for us by the time we get home."

He just perfectly encapsulated why I love him. The planning, the innate thoughtfulness, the slight cockiness in his assumption that we would be going home together. Not that I'm going to give him shit about that. I figure heroically saving my life and arranging to have the mess cleaned up earns him enough brownie points to get off that hook, permanently. The bonus of arranging for Emma Grace to be back home with us, well that earned him more than my good graces. It might even earn him actual lingerie from me.

"I love you."

I didn't mean to say it. It's not like it's a secret or like he doesn't know. Typically, we're not ones for saying it. We've always been the people who just showed it instead. But it's out there, and it honestly feels good.

132

He opens the front door and steps back to allow me to pass. "I know."

I glare at him. "Don't you Han Solo me, Clayton Darcy! I'm not pouring my heart out just so you can get cocky!"

"Fine. I love you," he says, opening the car door. But as I step past him to climb in, he crowds against me, until we're almost touching. I look up and he's staring down at me with the kind of intensity I would have found terrifying when I met him all those years ago. "But that's just a word...it doesn't even come close to describing everything I feel for you. When you're not in my life, it's like I can't breathe, like everything is just hollowed out and empty and all I'm doing is marking time till you come back."

Now *I* can't breathe. God above! How does he do that to me? How does he turn the tables and leave me just reeling from it all? "Damn you, Clayton."

"Get in the car, Annalee. Before we both bleed to death in the driveway."

CLAYTON

The adrenaline has worn off. It's just gone. I'm keeping my hands clenched into fists just so she can't see the fact that they're shaking. I've never been so fucking scared in all of my life.

If Samuel were in front of me right now, I'd hit the bastard again. A part of me wishes I had killed him. I know that he'll find some way to weasel out of this just because that's what he does.

Climbing behind the wheel, I start the engine and ease

onto the street. There are several people on their porches, a few curtains being drawn back as we drive by. Everyone in Fontaine wants to know what's going on and if we don't oblige them with information, they'll just make it up. Hell, they can't make up anything as deranged as the truth. I ought to let them.

That's a Mia question. She's the PR expert, so I'll let her do her thing and spin this in the way that is least damaging for the company and for those of us who have to continue living here.

The hospital is only a few minutes from the house. Everything in Fontaine is just a few minutes away, to be honest. I've seen more of this place in the last month than I ever want to again.

Walking in, I go to the desk and check us both in. The receptionist whose name I ought to know; hell, I think I went to high school with her mother, looks at me in absolute shock. I don't have to think hard to figure out why. Annalee and I both look like extras from a disaster movie. We're covered in blood, some of it our own, some of it Samuel's.

Handing over IDs and insurance cards, I take the forms she gives me and the two clipboards and go back to where Annalee is sitting. She chose a spot in the corner. *Like we can hide!*

"You're just going to have to brazen it out," I tell her. "Everyone in town is going to be talking about this...for a while. It's not going away quickly."

"Fantastic. Thanks for the pep talk," she sneers.

"Just keeping it real."

"That's my job," she says sharply. "Do you think this is going to make it weird for Emma Grace at school? And her big dance recital is tomorrow night...I don't want this insanity to overshadow it."

"We'll just make a bigger deal out of it to make sure it doesn't," I promise. And we will. I'd already planned on getting her flowers.

"What's going to happen to Samuel? Be honest with me here."

I sigh and stop filling out the form for a second. "He's not going to prison. It's a nice pipe dream, but you and I both know that won't happen."

"He broke in! He drugged me! He tried to kill me! He was planning to kill you and John!"

"But he's Samuel Darcy...and he has friends that will cover for him, that will call in favors. At the most, he's going to get a slap on the wrist in county jail. This will not be prosecuted to the fullest, Annalee...but he's still leaving here. Whatever it takes."

She's finished filling out her paperwork, so she takes the clipboard from me and starts filling out mine. She's the queen of multi-tasking. "I don't like it. I hate that he's getting away with it."

"He's not the only one who can call in favors...I can make his life hell here. And socially, after this, he's screwed. Most of his circle will drop him like a hot rock. It's not going to be hard to convince him to go."

"Promise me...I want him gone. If Emma Grace had been home—"

"Don't!" I can't think about it. I won't. If I do, I'll go find him and finish what I started. "I'm not letting anything happen to her. And I'm not letting anything else happen to you."

The ER door opens and a nurse appears. She calls Annalee back first and I sit there, waiting impatiently. I don't like that I can't lay eyes on her right now. Samuel is somewhere in the hospital, I know. I put nothing past the son of a bitch.

After a few minutes, the nurse calls for me. I walk toward her and she smirks. "So much for living on the hill. The Darcys have gone redneck."

I'm not in the mood. "Your brother works at the distillery...and your husband is trying to get a job there. Think you're helping out either of them right now?"

She clams up then, but her expression remains sour. I tolerate the temperature check, the invasive questions, and the blood pressure cuff that is way tighter than necessary. When she leads me back to the ER, she puts me in the cubicle next to Annalee's, not because she's being nice but because there's no other option. Samuel is on one side of the nurse's station and we're in the only two cubes on the other.

He's under guard. There are two sheriff's deputies standing outside the curtained-off area.

"I should have driven us to Lexington."

She looks over at me. "No. He's not running us off... not from here, not from anywhere. Besides, I've had a shitty day and I'm not dealing with that traffic."

I just want to be home. In my actual home...with my wife, with my daughter and without it looking like an earthquake zone. The doctor walks in and I just keep holding onto that thought.

Thirteen

ANNALEE

They finally discharged us both and I feel like we've been there for hours. I glance up at the clock as we're making our way outside and I realize we have actually been there for hours. Three of them, to be precise.

I look at Clayton over my shoulder. He looks exhausted and I know I don't look much better. "This day has been endless."

"Let's just go home. I want a shower...preferably with you and then I want to sleep for about twelve hours," he replies.

Heaven couldn't be better than that sounds. "No funny business in the shower. Neither one of us is allowed to get our stitches wet or do that much lifting."

"I'm probably too tired anyway," he says, and opens the car door for me. He kisses me and while it was intended to be a quick kiss, it doesn't stay that way. His lips move over mine and his tongue glides over the curve of my bottom lip. Resisting that is impossible. By the time he pulls back, we're both breathless and I can feel the heat pooling between my thighs. With nothing but a kiss, he makes me crazy.

"So much for sleeping," he says. "I've missed you. Every goddamn day, I've missed you."

"Just get me home and take me to bed. You can prove it."

The drive home is fast. Mia is sitting in the living room and Emma Grace is long since passed out in her bed. Mia looks from Clayton to me and then just shakes her head. "You both look like the walking dead."

I smile even though I don't really want to. I really want to yell at her to get the hell on out so he can rip my clothes off. Instead, I say, "We both kind of feel like it too."

Mia gets up off the couch and grabs her purse. "I can take a hint. I'll see you at Emma Grace's recital."

When she's gone, the door locked behind her, Clayton is on me instantly. His mouth is on my neck, his hands are stripping my clothes off.

"Emma Grace is upstairs," I protest.

"The office," he whispers. "The door locks."

It's also ten feet away. I move quickly and he's right behind me. The door closes softly and the clicking of the lock is impossibly loud. I'm already stripping.

I'm exhausted beyond belief. The events of the day have left me raw, like an exposed nerve. All the emotions are running hot and close to the surface, but I need this. I need him. To forget. To feel. To just escape into something blissful for a few minutes.

He's behind me, and I can feel his naked chest at my back as he guides me forward until I can lean over on the desk. His hands are on my back, stroking down over the curve of my hips, then cupping my ass. He pulls me up until I'm on my toes, my legs spread just a little. His hand slides between my thighs. I'm so wet for him already. I don't need any foreplay. Just him. Sinking into me. Filling me up.

"I need you," I whisper, and the sound is so broken I can barely recognize my voice.

"Tell me what you need, baby," he says softly and slips two fingers inside me. I arch my hips back against him, wanting more.

"Just fuck me...please. Don't make me wait. Don't make me beg."

I hear his zipper and then I feel him pressing against me, the velvety soft head brushing against my thighs. I press my forehead against the cool desktop and part my thighs just a bit wider. His breath hisses out, the sound so loud in the room. Then he's pushing into me, sinking in slowly.

I can feel every inch of him and I can't hold back the moan or the shiver. His fingers are gripping my hips tightly, digging into my flesh. He begins to move, withdrawing in long, slow strokes only to plunge in again, more forcefully, deeper. My whole body tenses in anticipation of that thrust, of the power and the heat of him.

One of his skilled and oh-so wicked hands moves from my hip, sliding over my belly, then lower until he's lightly strumming my clit in time with each thrust. I've got a death grip on the edge of the desk now and I can't hold back the shattered moans as he plays my body like an instrument.

My legs are trembling, the muscles of my thighs quivering as he strokes into me again and again. Everything inside me is coiled tight, the tension building to that razor edge between pleasure and pain. When his other hand moves up to my hair, gripping it tightly and pulling my head back, it simply snaps, the climax pulsing through me in time to the beat of my heart.

Clayton's movements become faster, rougher, and then he stiffens against, his hand clenching my hair even tighter. The flood of warmth as he comes inside me only heightens the tiny aftershocks of my own release, making me shiver beneath him.

When he leans forward and presses a kiss between my shoulder blades, I can't help but smile. There's always a contradiction in him, equal parts demanding and tender, gentle but with a firm touch. He is simply everything I have ever needed and more.

"We need a bed," he whispers. "Before we both fall over."

"You started it," I point out. He's moved away from me, and I immediately miss the warmth of him as I'm gathering my discarded clothes.

"You're kind of irresistible...and we've got some lost time to make up for," he says softly.

We do, but for now, all I want is to go to sleep with his arms wrapped around me. I want to wake up with his leg draped over, pinning me to the bed while I desperately try to figure out how to manage going to pee and not waking him up. It's funny the things you miss. The smell of his cologne, the fact that my side of the bed looked like a tornado had come through while his was barely disturbed, his often smart-ass remarks—all of those things have been missing from my life for a year, and now I get them back. It's overwhelming and I'm alternately grateful and terrified. I don't want to need him again, I don't want to be afraid of losing him again, but it's there, an incessant whisper in the back of my mind.

"Stop thinking," he says.

"Easy for you to say. I'm worried," I admit.

He's adjusted his clothes and looks moderately put together. I look like I've just been bent over a desk. "I'm worried—" It's a hard thing to confess, to put into words. "Worried this won't work. That somehow we're going to end up right back where we started...you'll be keeping secrets and I'll be jealous and insecure, wondering if it's another woman, or worse, and you just don't care anymore."

He pulls me into his arms, holding on to me tightly. I resent how right it feels. Yes, he's moving back in. Yes, the divorce has been called to a screaming halt. But we're not who we were a year ago, two years ago. This thing is still between us, a wall of solid ice over the parts of us that hurt the most. The only thing that will melt it is time, but if I can't get a handle on my fear and if I can't stop looking for all the ways it won't work, that's a chance we'll never get.

"Let's go to bed," I whisper. "I just can't think anymore tonight."

"It's going to be okay," he says softly.

"How do you know that?"

"Because I'll do whatever it takes to make it okay." His tone is firm despite the gentleness of his voice. It's so typical of him, but it makes me hopeful and I need that.

Fourteen

CLAYTON

There isn't much to pack at the condo. The furniture is all secondhand from either our basement or from Mama's. It's all so old and broken down it's not worth renting a truck to move it. I've dumped most of my clothes in suitcases. Annalee will probably find fault with how they're packed, and she probably should. But I don't care. I just want to be home. I want to officially be back in my own home and have this shithole in my rearview mirror.

The knock at the door is a surprise. I wasn't expecting anyone. To see John standing there, I know something is up. "What's he done?" I ask immediately.

"He wants to make a deal," John replies evenly. "And my expert opinion is that you ought to go along with it."

"Did you miss the part where he tried to murder my wife?" I ask. I know he's not going to prison for it. I know that somehow he will get out of it, but it pisses me off.

"He's never going to trial, Clayton. We both know

that. The DA is married to the daughter of Samuel's golfing partner, who also happens to be the judge who would preside over this case." I can tell John is pissed. He only ever gets all lawyerly and chatty when he's mad as hell. "That's assuming we could get a grand jury to even indict him in a county where everyone is terrified, in debt, or otherwise beholden to your damn father in some way."

"So that's it?" I demand. "We're not even going to try? This would ruin him forever, John. Completely!"

John shoves his hand into his hair. "At what cost? You, your wife, your kid...you still have to live in this town. Is it better to ruin him and have everyone at your kid's school know about it or to let him go quietly and preserve some dignity?"

It's true and I know it, but I don't like it. Still, Annalee and Emma Grace have to come first. "What does he want?"

"To talk to you," John replies. "They took him from the hospital to the jail this morning, but he won't be there for long. They've already called the judge to get bail set for him."

"It's Saturday morning!"

"Like it or not, people owe your daddy, Clayton, and they will move heaven and earth for him."

I throw the rest of the clothes in the last suitcase and carry it out to the car. John's waiting for me there. I'm not stupid enough to talk to Samuel alone. That would bite me in the ass for sure.

The drive to the jail is short. I'm not saying anything and neither is he. I'm pissed off all over again. The idea of setting eyes on him reignited the fury from the day before.

"Do not lose it in here! For someone who spent his whole life being the calm one, you've lost your damn mind!" John cautions.

It's true. I was the calm one, but the last year has changed all that. We head into the jail and go through the ridiculous process of getting screened to visit the prisoner. After it's done, we're shown to a small room with a table and a few chairs that are clearly held over from the'70's.

Samuel's face is busted all to hell. His nose is broken, both eyes black and his lip is split. It's more satisfying than I thought it would be to see him that way.

"You wanted to talk. Talk." I'm not going to spend my whole damn day listening to his demands when I have no desire to meet any of them.

"I want the million dollars you promised...in writing, in a binding contract. If you'll do that, when they let me out of here, I'm gone," he offers.

"That deal is off the table," I insist. "You lost your bargaining power when you tried to kill my wife."

"I could always try again," Samuel says softly. "You work an awful lot, Clayton. You leave that poor woman alone too much."

I want to murder him, to ram my fucking fist into his face so hard that he'll never get up again. "If you ever go near her again—"

"Let's not be hasty," John butts in. "Don't say anything in here that you might regret later."

"I won't regret it."

"As your lawyer," he insists, "I can promise you that you will. When do you want the money?"

"As soon as the trust comes through," Samuel says. "And whatever is in the account right now is all mine."

There's nothing in that account. The last of his expenses came through and wiped it out. "You're sure we can't get this to stick?" I ask.

John shakes his head. "A million dollars is a small price to pay if it means being rid of him forever."

I know he's right. The good ol' boy system is still alive and well in Kentucky. It doesn't matter how open and shut the evidence in a case is, if it's never permitted to go to trial. If it came down to it, those crooked bastards would just keep issuing continuances until the son of a bitch kicks the bucket.

"I agree to the terms, but I have a few of my own. If..." I am staring him dead in the eye as I say it. "You ever step foot back in the state or attempt contact with any member of our family, the contract is void. Not only is it void, but I will take you to civil court for all that you've done. The criminal court judge and the DA might be in your pocket, but I've got friends of my own that you can't touch."

Samuel grins, the expression grotesque on his swollen and bruised lips. "You'll never admit it, but you're just like me, Clayton."

It's not entirely true, but there are enough similarities that I'm not going to argue the point. It'd be an exercise in futility anyway.

"Get the papers drawn up, John. I'll sign them and then I don't ever want to set eyes on this fucker again."

I walk out of the small room and it feels like I can breathe again. I've always hated him, even when I was a kid. I can remember seeing Mama cry, again and again... over the infidelity, over his cruelty. Emotional abuse wasn't something I could conceptualize then, but as an adult, I know that's what he did to her. It's what he did to all of us.

John walks out just a minute behind me. "You know that's all bullshit, right?"

"What?"

"You're not like him, Clayton," John says. "You might bend the rules, you might even break them...but you didn't do it because you felt they just didn't apply to you.

You did it because that was the only way to bring him down. The problem we have right now is that not a damn one of us recognized just how bat-shit crazy he really is."

"Let's hope it's not genetic." The joke falls flat. But having just agreed to give him a million dollars of the money that is supposed to be used to take care of Mama, neither one of us is in the mood for humor.

"You need to get Quentin and Mia to agree to this," he says. "I don't think they'll balk when they know why. But still, based on the guardianship agreement he signed yesterday, it has to be all three of you or it's a no go."

"I'll see Mia tonight...I'll talk to Quentin tomorrow. It'll be taken care of by Monday."

John nods. "In the meantime, don't leave Annalee alone. I wouldn't put it past him to try something again."

After that, I drop John back at the condo where his car is parked and head home. Annalee is waiting with Emma Grace to go to her dance recital. I promised her I wouldn't miss it for the world and I meant every word.

"You don't look happy," Annalee says.

Total honesty is a bitch. I glance in the rearview mirror. Emma Grace has her little pink iPod out and her earphones in. "We're going to have to pay Samuel to leave town, otherwise, he just hangs around like a bad smell, and we'll never be rid of him."

"Out of Patricia's trust?" she asks.

"Yes. That's pretty much all we have unless Quentin comes through with an investor. He might...it could be a big turning point for all of us financially."

She nods, and then she simply lays her hand over top of mine. I turn my palm up and twine my fingers through hers.

"I trust you. You'll do what's best for all of us...you always do, even if I don't approve of your methods."

"No more secrets. No more lies...in the meantime, I'm stuck to you like glue."

She grins. "I like the sound of that."

It feels like it used to, for just a moment, at least. "We're really okay, aren't we?"

"We're getting there," she says. "It's not a straight line back to the top, Clayton. There's going to be fits and starts. There will be days when I'm still mad, days when I question everything you say and everything you don't."

"I love you...and if that means tolerating abuse from you on occasi—"

She pulls her hand from mine and glares at me. "Abuse? Really?"

I snatch her hand back. "I'll do penance later," I promise.

"We're supposed to have dinner at your mama's with Mia and Bennett tomorrow. Quentin's coming...and Mia told me she's bringing someone you'll want to meet."

"Who?" I ask.

"Your half brother," Annalee says softly.

I knew. Not his name or his location or his age, but I knew he existed. "When did she meet him?"

"This morning...he's from Ireland. Your dad definitely got around. And apparently he and Loralei Crawford are a thing."

"He came all the way to Kentucky and hooked up with his half sister's best friend?" I ask. It sounds fishy.

"Don't borrow trouble," she warns. "You don't know anything about him yet...and stranger things have happened. You met me dancing around a burning couch and told me on our first date you were going to marry me."

"What's so strange about that?" I ask.

"I didn't run away screaming."

I glance back at Emma Grace who is singing blissfully out of tune in the back seat. "You can try that later. I promise to catch you."

"I love you," she says. "Even when I was mad as hell at you, I loved you. And I don't ever want to be without you again."

"You won't. That's another promise I'm going to keep."

The Beginning

CLAYTON

It's five in the morning and I'm still wide awake. I'm in the passenger seat of my car, looking up through the sunroof that always leaks, as the first light of dawn starts to filter through. I'm more than awake. I feel completely alive and it's because of the girl beside me.

"Tell me about your family," she says.

"I already told you," I say.

"Tell me again. I like hearing about them."

I turn my head to look at her. Somehow, with mind boggling flexibility, she's curled up on her side in the driver's seat with her legs tucked beneath her. "My mom will like you...when you're ready to meet her. My dad... not so much. But he doesn't like anybody, so fuck him."

She smiles. "Tell me about your brother and sister...I always wanted siblings. It sucked being an only child."

"Quentin...he's just an asshole. A total smart-ass, but he plays football like nobody I've ever seen. He's really

149

good. And girls love him, for a little while anyway. He invariably pisses them off and then they go psycho on him."

"Is that a family trait? Are you going to do something so bad that I turn into one of those crazy women they make TV movies about?"

Now it's my turn to laugh. I'd have to be an idiot to fuck this up. "No. I'm not doing that...and I don't really want to talk about my family anymore. I want to hear about yours."

She looks up at the sunroof. "There's not a whole lot to tell. It's just me. I don't have a family."

"What do you mean you don't have a family?"

A shrug of her shoulders is all I get for the longest time. "I don't know my father. I don't even know his name...no siblings. My mother died two years ago. So, it's just me."

I can't imagine being that alone. The idea of it terrifies me. "I'm so sorry."

"I'm not. My mom wasn't really....wel, when she had drugs, she ignored me. When she didn't have drugs, I wished she would ignore me. Trust me when I tell you that I'm totally okay with not having her in my life anymore. I hate that she wasted her life the way she did, but it's a relief to not have her wasting anymore of mine."

The silence in the car is overwhelming. The weight of what she just said is tangible. Yes, my father is an asshole and he makes everyone around him miserable, but we still have my mother and she keeps that in check. She's made sure that we always had what we needed and that she was always there for us. And this amazing girl has had no one.

"Now that we're both depressed," she says with a self-deprecating laugh. "I do actually need to go. I have to work today. And if I leave now, I can get a total of five hours of sleep before I have to be at the restaurant."

It's selfish but I'm not ready to let her go yet. "Just a few more minutes?"

She sits up in the seat and, in one fluid motion that I can't begin to comprehend, climbs over the console until she's straddling my thighs, her mouth just inches from mine. "I have to go...but don't you think you should at least try to kiss me first?"

"I want to do a hell of a lot more than kiss you but I'm trying to show off how much of a gentleman I can be."

"I'd rather you show me what it's like when you stop being a gentleman." Her voice is pitched low, sexy as hell, and impossible to resist.

I slide one hand beneath the hem of her skirt, over the satin skin of her thigh and then the curve of her hip. She's not wearing any panties. If there was any blood in my body going anywhere but to my cock, it just changed direction.

"So is this no panties thing a policy you have or just a pleasant surprise?" I ask.

"I hate panties. I avoid them at all costs," she says. "But do you really want to talk about my underwear right now?"

She never wears panties. I've been sitting next to her all night long and she's had not a stitch on under that skirt. "You're trying to kill me, aren't you?"

She leans forward slightly, until her lips are less than a breath from mine. "No. You're no good to me that way."

I honestly think I'll die if I don't kiss her. Placing my other hand in her hair, I wrap my fist in it and tug her just a little closer, until her mouth is on mine. The softness of her lips, the taste of her when I lick the curve of her lower lip is enough to make me crazy.

Her lips part on a soft, little sigh and the kiss deepens, takes on a life of its own. She kisses like sin. Like everything that is so bad for you but feels so goddamn good.

She rocks her hips slightly and I can feel the heat of her even through the jeans I'm wearing. We're dry humping in a car like a couple of horny teenagers and it's the best moment of my life.

I shift my hand beneath her skirt, moving it between her thighs and meeting nothing but bare, slick skin. God above.

She breaks the kiss and I'm almost certain she's about to tell me no. "We could take this inside," she offers. "My apartment isn't much bigger than this car and my bed is also my couch, but at least it's private."

If I do what she expects me to, if I have sex with her here in the front seat of this car or if I follow her into her apartment, I'll never see her again. So as much as it kills me, I'm not going to get what I want today. But I'll make sure she does. "If I go in with you, we both know what will happen."

She grins. "That's kind of why I'm inviting you in."

"And that's why I'm saying no...because I'm not going to be a one-night stand. Not with you," I tell her.

"So you like me too much to have sex with me?" she asks dubiously.

"That sums it up," I reply. "I want to see you again. And when I'm sure you're not going to bolt, then we'll spend the night at my apartment."

"Why yours?"

"Because I have a king-size bed and we can cover every inch of it," I answer.

She looks at me for a long moment, clearly puzzled, and then says, "That is a compelling argument...so if we're not going to have sex, you should probably move your hand."

I do, but not in the way she intended. I slip my fingers inside her, gently grazing her clit. "I'm not going to have sex...I'm saving myself. But that doesn't mean we both have to suffer."

ANNALEE

When I first met him at that party, I thought he was just another rich, frat boy. But he was so hot I was willing to overlook it. Then he convinced me to go to breakfast with him. Now, I'm sitting across his lap in the front seat of his car and he's doing things with his fingers that have melted every bone in my body.

I don't know what to make of Clayton Darcy. He's not who I thought he'd be and that scares me to death. "What's your game?" I ask him. My voice is breathless, husky, and I can't keep the tremor out of it as he touches me.

"I don't have one," he says and his fingers move deeper, pressing inside me in a way that takes my breath away. I grip his shoulders because it's the only way I can stay upright. "I want to make you come. Then tonight, I'm going to be at the Green Lantern at closing time to pick you up. I'll take you to breakfast again." He kisses my neck, then my collarbone, the gentle glide of his tongue on my skin and the thrusting of his hand between my thighs is more than I can take.

"I don't know what you want from me," I whisper, but it ends on a moan as his thumb brushes over my clit.

"I want you to say yes," he tells me.

"To what?"

He smiles and shifts his hand slightly. Every muscle in my body goes tense. I'm hovering on the edge and he knows it. "To whatever I ask you for."

He's still moving inside me, curling his fingers in a way that makes my whole body quake. Those gentle brushes of his thumb over my clit are perfect torture. "Clayton, for the love of God! Are you trying to make me beg?"

He dips his head and places a kiss between my breasts and then turns slightly to take one nipple between his teeth. It's just the right amount of pressure, that perfect balance between pleasure and pain. Couple with the slow deliberate movements of his hand between my thighs, I fall. There's no other way to describe it. All the tension in my body holding me upright simply vanishes and I collapse against him, trembling.

I've had orgasms, more often on my own than not, but nothing like this where it just goes on and on. My thighs are quaking and I can't catch my breath as he continues to play me like an instrument.

"Stop...please, stop." I am begging now. It's too much.

He kisses me again, gently, his lips moving over mine as if I were something precious. No one has ever kissed me that way. No man has ever made me come without getting his own.

As he withdraws his hand, I shiver and his arms close around me.

"You're dangerous," I tell him.

"Why do you say that?"

I look at him then, at the green eyes that seem so sincere. "Because you make me believe in things I shouldn't, and that could break my heart."

"I won't do that," he says. "That's the last thing I ever want to do."

I need to be away from him, just to clear my head. Opening the door, I climb out of the car and try to ignore the fact that my knees are wobbling like I've been on a three day drunk.

"I will see you tonight, Annalee," he insists. "You can count on it."

God, I hope so.

CLAYTON

I should go back to the apartment and survey the damage from the party I abandoned. But my roommate is probably passed out and he's more than likely invited some random couple to fuck like rabbits in my bed. I don't want to deal with that. I don't want to deal with a bunch of drunk, hungover assholes puking all over the place.

On the north side of town, I'm just as close to Fontaine as I am to my apartment near campus. It's almost six by now. By the time I get there, Mama will be up, and like every mama's boy ever born, I have the overwhelming urge to go home to her.

I put the car in drive and take the familiar route. I could drive it in my sleep, and considering I haven't seen a bed in around twenty-four hours, that's a good thing.

Parking at the back of the house, I walk into the kitchen and she's sitting at the counter having her first cup of coffee and scouring her cookbooks.

"Who are you trying to impress?" I ask, leaning against the refrigerator.

"You look like something the cat dragged in. Have you even been to bed?" she demands.

"Not yet," I answer. I don't lie to her. I can't. She always sees straight through me. "I'll crash in a minute."

"Why are you here, Clayton? It's either something really good or really bad to have you standing in my kitchen at this time of morning," she surmises.

"It's good. I met the girl I'm going to marry." It's a crazy thing to say, and I honestly didn't intend to say it. But it's out there. No doubts or second guesses. I knew it the moment I laid eyes on her.

Mama rolls her eyes and laughs. "Please tell me you didn't say that to her!"

Now I'm rolling my eyes. "I'm not crazy. She'd bolt. I'll just bide my time and ease her into the idea...by the way, Samuel will hate her on sight."

"He hates everybody. How is that news?"

It's not a secret that their marriage sucks, that he's a cheating bastard. I've never asked the question, but now I have to. "Why do you stay with him?"

She sips her coffee and considers her answer carefully. "I don't plan to for much longer. This town is so small... and everything we do is under scrutiny. When Mia has finished high school and gone off to college and doesn't have to stay here with every busybody in Fontaine digging at her, then I'm going to divorce him."

"Please tell me you plan to hire a shark for an attorney and take every last penny he has?"

Mama laughs. "He's got fewer pennies than anyone realizes. The money, Clayton, is mine. It always was. We'll see how many of those pretty, young blondes are still interested in him then, won't we?"

The word divorce in reference to one's parents ought

to prompt fear or dread or sadness. In this instance, it's just relief. "We'll have a party."

"No, we will not. You have partied enough," she says. "Go to bed before you fall over and when you get up, you can tell me all about this girl."

I leave the kitchen and head upstairs to my old room. It feels good to be home and to know that in a few short hours, I'll be seeing Annalee again.

A Special Sneak Peek at Carter

BOURBON & BLOOD BOOK THREE

The truck's powerful engine rumbled as Clayton Darcy extricated himself from the back seat. He was drunk off his ass and they'd probably all hear about tomorrow from Mia and Annalee, Carter thought. If anyone had told him that he'd be out drinking with a Darcy, much less with the rest of the Hayes clan with him, he'd have called them a damn liar.

But his mind wasn't really on Clayton or even on the game they'd just watched while consuming excessive amounts of beer and more than their fair share of shots. It was her. She was in his fucking head, mixing it all up and making him crazy. It had been like that from day one and he was tired of it.

He glanced over toward her house. It was one of the smaller homes in the subdivision where Clayton Darcy lived. It had been hell sneaking around in that neighborhood and trying not to be seen, but again, that had been her choice. She was the one who wanted to hide, who wanted to pretend like they were nothing to each other.

The light was on upstairs in her bedroom. Was she in

bed reading one of the smutty novels she liked? Or was she watching some sappy TV show while eating ice cream? He knew her habits, he knew so much about her, and yet in public, they'd never shared more than a few words.

Clayton stumbled up the driveway and managed to get himself into the house. Emmitt, the only one of them still sober, shifted the truck into drive. It surged forward but had gone no more than fifty feet before Carter yelled out. "Stop the truck!"

"You puke in here and I'm gonna kick your ass!" Emmitt shouted.

"Just let me out, dammit!" Carter replied.

Bennett shifted forward in his seat and Carter moved past him through the open door. He crossed the road and marched toward her front door. He was done with hiding. She wanted him to be some big secret, something on the side while she played the good girl in front of the whole town. He was done with that shit.

Raising his fist, he pounded on the door. "Josie! I know you're in there!"

In the truck, Bennett looked at Emmitt. "Did you know about this?"

"Ain't that Josie Marcum's house?" Emmitt shot back. "What the hell would she be doing with Carter?"

Bennet raised his eyebrow. "What do all women do with Carter?"

"True enough...but Josie Marcum? Hell."

They watched him walking up to her door. Bennett asked, "Should we wait for him?"

"Hell no!" Emmitt said. "I'm not sitting outside waiting for his ass while he gets laid!"

"We don't know that he's getting laid!" Bennett protested.

Emmitt made a noise of complete derision. "It's Carter and she's female. Hell, she'll probably greet him pussy first."

"Jesus, you're crude!" Bennett said with a shake of his head.

"Yeah, well, I'm not in love so I don't have to pretty it all up," Emmitt said and eased the truck into drive. "She can drive his ass home when she's done with him."

On the porch, Carter was preparing to bang on the door again, when the porch light suddenly flicked on. The door opened a crack, and he could see Josie peering out at him.

"What are you doing here?" she hissed at him.

"Open the damn door and let me in!" he barked.

"I will not!"

"If you don't," he replied, "I will stand out here making so damn much noise one of your uptight neighbors will call the cops. It'll be all over town by morning, Josie, that I got arrested on your doorstep!"

Her eyes widened. "You wouldn't dare."

Carter smiled, but it wasn't a friendly expression. There was none of his usual charm in it. Instead it was mean and even a little vicious. "You ought to know better than anybody that there's not a lot I won't do. Now open the damn door!"

The door closed and he heard the lock click and the chain slide free. When she opened it and stepped back, he didn't hesitate, but just barged in slamming the door behind him.

"What do you think you're doing?" she demanded. "Do you have any idea what people are saying?"

"The truth?" he asked. "That I've been sneaking over here and fucking you on an almost nightly basis? That I make you scream and beg and say the kind of words that would have everybody at the First Baptist Church praying for your soul?"

She rolled her eyes heavenward. "Just because I don't want to trot my business out for everyone in town *or* be lumped in with all the other women you string along—"

"String along?" he demanded. He was so angry he wanted to shake her. Instead, he ran his fingers through his hair in a gesture of frustration and annoyance. "Since I bumped into you in that damn bar in Cincinnati I haven't had time for a conversation with another woman, much less the time string one along! And if anyone's doing any stringing here, it's you!"

"Me? I don't think so, Carter Hayes. You're welcome to walk anytime you want to...that's all this is anyway. Just a little bit of fun, right? Isn't that what you said?"

"Oh, yeah. This is so much fun!" he snarked. It was fun like ramming your face into a brick wall. He started to walk out. Hell, he wasn't even sure why he came there. It had been a beer-fueled impulse and now he wasn't sure if he regretted it or not. He glanced back at her. She was clearly mad as hell. Her arms were crossed over her chest and her chin was up. But it was the look of hurt and disappointment in her eyes that made him stop. He'd known she could hurt him. She had more times already than he could count. But he'd never thought, not even for a second, that he had the power to hurt her.

"Fuck it," he whispered and turned back to her. He grasped her wrist, tugging her forward until she was pressed against him. She wore nothing or next to nothing beneath the robe she had on. His hands went to her hair immediately, tugging her head back until she was looking up at him. Her lips were parted, not in surprise, but anticipation. Lowering his mouth to hers, he kissed her, his lips moving over hers with all the urgency that he felt. He didn't want to lose her, but he wasn't going to take the scraps either.

Sliding his tongue between her lips, the kiss took on a note that was blatantly carnal. He wasn't even sure how it happened, but suddenly her back was against the wall and her legs were wrapped around his waist. His cock was so hard he thought it might literally kill him, and she was moaning into his mouth. Drawing back, Carter looked at her, at the flush in her cheeks and her kiss swollen lips. Without a drop of makeup on her face, she was the most beautiful woman he'd ever laid eyes on. If he unzipped his pants, he could be inside her in less than ten seconds. And he was going to walk away.

"I'm not doing this with you anymore, Josie...you want to fuck me, then you're going to have to date me."

"Excuse me?" she said, blinking at him in confusion.

"You heard me," he said. "If you want me in your bed, then you're going to be seen with me...in public." He stepped back, and her legs unlocked from his waist until she was standing on her own two feet. "You know where to find me."

Carter opened the door and walked out into the night. Bennett and Emmitt were long gone. It wouldn't be the first time he'd walked home, probably wouldn't be the last, because he didn't believe for a second that Josie Marcum would ditch her good girl image to slum it with him.

AVAILABLE AUGUST 2025

Chasity Bowlin is a *USA Today* bestselling author of numerous romance novels. She resides in central Kentucky with her husband, their charming son, and a lively menagerie of animals. A passionate traveler, Chasity enjoys weaving glimpses of her real-life adventures into her stories. As an avid Anglophile, she adores all things British, with a particular love for the Regency era.

Born and raised in Tennessee, Chasity spent much of her childhood with her doting grandparents, where soap operas and back-to-back episodes of Scooby-Doo were part of her daily routine. Her path to becoming a romance novelist was perhaps inevitable—her Barbie dolls didn't just cruise in pink convertibles; they traveled through time, hosted extravagant dinner parties, and one even had an evil twin locked in the attic.

www.chasitybowlin.com